T0156640

Treason's Truth

Mac Alpin's Scotland

Jeffrey Underwood
and
Kate Taylor

iUniverse, Inc.
Bloomington

TREASON'S TRUTH
MAC ALPIN'S SCOTLAND

iUniverse books may be ordered through booksellers or by contacting:

iUniverse
1663 Liberty Drive
Bloomington, IN 47403
www.iuniverse.com
1-800-Authors (1-800-288-4677)

ISBN: 978-1-4759-3194-5 (sc)
ISBN: 978-1-4759-3195-2 (ebk)

Library of Congress Control Number: 2012910262

Printed in the United States of America

iUniverse rev. date: 06/18/2012

Contents

NOT FOR EIGHTEEN AND UNDER

Introduction

This slice of historical fiction begins with the ancient vampire entity of The Forbidden Tome; Hansel and Gretel's True Tale and of Lethal Assumed; Lost Tome Found, not in Germany of the 1850s or present day Seattle but in the days of yore when Scotland was in its womb and about to be birthed.

The tale of Cinaed Mac Alpin, known commonly as Kenneth, and his queen Aiobheean opens as his life is fledgling and he is a boy of seven in 818AD British Isles. So much is primitive but moving towards formation of a nation.

The scale of the story is huge. And yes, it involves vampires and passionate embraces of significant characters in history. Yet the book also includes the sweep of one hundred and forty critical years in the building of that romantic land they now call Scotland.

Have you ever wondered about what truly ensued with the incident known as Mac Alpin's Treason? Or with the clash of the Pictish and Gael cultures and with how the Pictish way of life vanished? Where did those tattooed people go? Or with how the Catholic Church brought its weight upon the land? Find answers, sophisticated answers, in this rendering.

There are descriptions of the people who allowed this time to flow down upon the world. There are births, deaths, passion, sadness and the tumultuous turmoil of a bold but wild era.

Sink your teeth into this tale.

Acknowledgments

My Marvel & Coauthor Kate Taylor
Penny Woodward my continuing muse
Ellie Mackay
Sweet Judith
Chris Bebee
Cinaed (Kenneth) Mac Alpin
Scotland
Stephanie W. who taught us that you are never too old
to feel the tug of love at your heartstrings.
Maureen Hovenkotter who introduced me
to the Treason.
To the publisher who made the telling possible

CHAPTER 1

Destiny's Ride

For approximately six hundred years, he dwelt in isolation in the dark holes interspersed as oft snowless crevices and naturally bored bleak uamhs in Am Monadh. From afar, over these years, he had taken note of the progress of the several clashing tribes which often stirred violently at the base of his massive and indestructible hideaway.

He had been waiting over half a millennium since his previous incarnation for the correct human spirit to inhabit. He was simmering to shed his separation and ride the wave of human culture once again. His destiny this round was at imminent creation and he was profoundly excited at the prospect.

Anonymity had served him decently for the span he had just spent in the frigid mountains here. Of course he had fed; but it was primarily on detestably poor quality blood. Animals yielded enough for him to survive but humans allowed him to thrive. He was simply bristling with an almost uncontrolled anticipation; almost uncontrolled, as he truly controlled most everything within his sphere.

He had been restless shortly after dispensing with Septimius in the tumbling years of Roman decline all about the world. Restless then was mild in comparison and not what galvanized his senses in this moment; it was a huge surge that pierced his spirit to almost frantic impending motion. He hunkered down in the dank and dripping tunnel that he had considered home for far too long. He was clenching himself tighter and tighter as he prepared to recoil and exit the cave. He was unable to resist the primal call that wrapped its tentacles around him. This was not his power of foresight, which was much limited and rudimentary. No, this was the wrenching force of an essence beyond him. It was pulling him, silently screaming in his head to fly now. All that he knew absolutely was that his instincts were to be his only guide for an unknown length.

This vast compulsion had played upon his history before. And he had blindly followed it as he would do this time too. What embodiment then did he have to anticipate now in the arms of this nameless weave upon him and a brutish era surrounding him?

He rushed to the sky and converted into the winged form that he loathed but that allowed him to gobble up distances as he thrashed the air mercilessly. He was not likely to return ever to his den and for that he was thankful to be plying the clouds and caressing the moon's sliver as he shot forward toward horizons of mystery and import.

All that he ascertained in this moment of exit from prior shelter and entry into history's precipice was that he was to enjoin with one who was to impact mankind's trajectory forward. He had known two other pivotal periods in his craven life; one tethered to the dawn of time and the other bound to the flailing of the Roman Empire. His impact had been irregular and he was ready for better. He had been an icon of chaos and destruction as the son of Cain, Mezopx. Septimius had brought no ultimate harm to the human species at least, had restored Roman buildings but he had hardly been an individual to leave much more than ventures that had been undergirded by violence and war. He pleaded for a human skin that was to bestow more significant influence upon primitives yearning to be led. He further pondered though that he knew not where his pleas fell. So, he had no certainty of whether the spirit driving him cared about his desires. This force was greater than him and it placed him seemingly wherever it chose. In spite, he begged in case it meant anything.

He continued to swirl in the river of stained dark clouds with palpitation of pulse grown all consuming. His wingspan insured that he jockeyed these heavens with disregard for his safety. His flap of wings was so hard churning that an ability to remain aloft no matter the conditions was his to assert always. And the conditions experienced this dense enshrouded night was eerily calm besides. He felt hardly a burst or brush of air as he swept over the retreating mountainous landscape to more benign flattened wilderness. Small encampments hewn out of lessening timber were espied by him as he followed magnetically that mysterious dominion which was directing the beat of his heavy appendages through the air.

As he hurtled downward toward an oblong circular patch of fire lit illumination, the earlier shrieks that commanded him from inside his skull to become airborne and search out a different destination softened. Somehow, he recognized that this quieting was his compass. The closer he came to his target the more diminished the cacophony inside his brain became. Thus he dropped swiftly toward what was a fortress and city within that fortress. His mind was almost his own again so proximate was he to the male that he was about to transform to.

The walls of stone surrounding the enclave and the wheelhouses intermixed with roundhouses were well laid and large but had no effect on his entry as he swooped lower. He then shot through one sodded roof no different than the sodded roofs of the neighboring houses and met his fate in the form of a large built, pale skinned, brownish haired sleeping male. Molecules of his collided with molecules of this other and instant fusion occurred. He was this man until that guiding force instructed him otherwise.

He knew now exactly where he was and who he was. His resting place was in one called Eumann. He roused this Eumann, in order to rise and find the way to undead tomb of enough quality to thoroughly shelter himself from the coming sun's potentially damning toxicity. He was to learn the ways of the clan that he had just joined and the burgeoning culture that he was to contribute to vastly. First though, he had to find shelter for his being from the scorched effect of the sun's rays upon him. These people were going to have to adapt to his presence in eventide only. That was to be the way of it from this instant forward.

They were to yield to his requirements, as Eumann was also the tutor for the very youthful Cinaed. His vampire overseer left a full mapping so that there was immediate understanding of land and person surrounding him.

If he had done this at Cinaed's birth, he would have traversed over open sea to the island of Iona. But Cinaed was now the proud owner of seven years of breath and experience. He was a rambunctious and rowdy lad with an intellect that soaked in so much so rapidly. Eumann was to teach and guard over this youngster. This youngster was special and therefore Eumann's instructions to the boy were outsize and deeply significant as well.

But he also comprehended magically that much had stirred and changed since Cinaed's birth. The family no longer tended the desolate treeless terrain of the island of his origin but instead had risked the sweep of ocean to alight in the territory of Dal Riata. Eumann was blessed to be profoundly attached to Cinaed's father, a clan warrior and near King of the locale, and to Cinaed's mother, Pictish princess and dark beauty of magnificent spirit.

Time, in human terms, was about eight hundred years after the coming of Christ.

CHAPTER 2

Love's Fool

Up and outside, just as he was readying himself to search for an adequate lair, Eumann froze at the subtle touch of hand to his shoulder. This touch hardened into a firmer grip and he moved to peer into Catrione's shining eyes.

"You dash off at such odd and stealthy hours my favorite tutor. Might you rather share a string of moments with me? Teach me the means to fan your flame. That is my heart's desire. I assumed that it was yours also."

Eumann paused to absorb what was a blatant invitation to find combined pleasure with this woman. He calculated the period prior to dawn's rude arrival and decided quickly that there were ample hours to dally; he had most certainly dallied with this enchantress on earlier occasions. And he was primed, ready and anxious to engage with her on the instant; it had been so long with anyone. And that was even if not all of Eumann's character traits fell into place perfectly yet. He was prepared to enchant her so deliciously that she was to be willing to gloss over those tiny irregularities of his. Eumann was to be all that she would covet and then some!

"You hesitate as if you are unable to answer me. What is your reply to my not easily shared confession to you?"

Her hand belied her difficulty in revealing anything to him as she let it drop to his wool covered manhood and compressed his just now rousing cock and nestled sack. He covered her smooth, warm, soft rhythmically squeezing hand with his own large hand and by that encouraged her further movements.

He had spoken nary a word yet but was about to straightaway in a whispered hush. "Fair Catrione, lush and lovely princess of Fortrenn's house, I crave embracing you; yet I fear it here in the open, though the shadows wrap us tightly. Even our hands as they are make me cautious, though very aroused simultaneously. Do know that, yes, you stir all parts of me, heart and soul foremost, and it has been thus always. Let us please go from here and take me now to our nest. I need to be able to touch you freely."

They unclasped at interlocked fingers and pulled their hands from his bulge. He watched as the luster of her magnificent emerald irises picked up more light out of what little was proffered from the opaque night. He read the subtle changes in her eyes and knew that she was excited. Her pupils dilated as they maintained their gaze upon one another. Every clue of her sentiment aided him in his approach to her here.

Soon enough his own visionary abilities, though still rough and not remotely as evolved as they would be in the future, were to make his task of incorporating into Eumann's personal life effortless. That time was to take a while, months possibly. His impatience and irritation were often the very facts that made his progress that much slower. His calming attempts were primitive and only partially successful to say the least. He was to learn a more temperate approach with practice. His manifest abilities were to enlarge fantastically over the eons as he absorbed the notion that settled energy worked much better for him and his goals.

A vampire's sexual appetite became ravenous once sparked. His was that and he yielded to it and Catrione's evident excitement. He trailed her once she stepped toward the maze of houses before them. Even as the undead, he was smitten with her already. She was bold, for sure. He did not find that unappealing at all. He enjoyed his sexual partners as ferocious and large in their own appetites as he was. Regarding his victims, well, that was an altogether different matter.

What he gleaned as he viewed her from behind was valued for its reflection of who she was as a person but was also a goad to his filling cock as she stimulated his senses intensely. She was short of stature. And though he lusted after all gorgeous female forms, he was most enamored of women who combined lessened height yet prominent chest. He craved that contrast as it created illusion of even larger breast than was true. Was that to be? He stifled his powers and did not caress her curves mentally. He desired surprise.

What further had he garnered of her? Though she was mostly hidden by her long and hooded woolen cloak, he had noted much. Her hair had gently rested upon her forehead in clusters of dark ringlets below raiment's border upon his first glance. Her skin was a very sensuous pale cream color that was smooth upon high lifted cheekbones. Her lips were ripe and plump. Her eyebrows were thick and lush. Her radiating green eyes were set perfectly above a small and slimly aquiline nose. And in spite of layered clothing for the chill of a tranquil yet icy nightfall, her highborn status was apparent to him easily. The intricate copper brooch that she had clasped to her closed cloak was thick and luminous. Only the wealthy and politically important Picts were permitted this extravagance in ornamentation.

The soft fluctuations of her curvaceous buttocks were delicately evident through the material that flared slightly below her waist. He discerned that her poise and fluidity here expressed a woman of great carnality. Her seamless gait forward revealed to him the further detail that she and Eumann had travelled this route often before. Her stride bespoke a familiarity with this routine quite clearly.

Since she did not pause at all, that gave him additional indication that she hurried somewhat in fear of discovery. Really though, it was that vision beyond his own, that vision that led him to Eumann, which informed him of the fact that she was married to, not the king, but the lieutenant for this territory and enclave. Presently, this very warrior-soldier was fighting combatants from Strathclyde. Prior, he had warred with the very Picts whose clan Catrione hailed from. She had been captured by her husband, Alpin Mac Eachaide, in an altogether different battle a dozen years back and had adapted well to her new set of circumstances. She cherished the greater security of this tribe over her original Pictish one but that did not lend itself to similarly cherishing her husband. She did not.

If Eumann and Catrione were found in joined intimacy, both he and she had no recourse but to submit to the fierce discipline that the heathen warrior council would determine. This sort of infidelity, especially with a near-lord being cuckolded while fighting for the sake of the tribe, would go severely for them. Alpin was likely to be appointed to mete out their punishment. And in his wrath, they surely would be slowly and savagely put to death. Of course, Eumann did not dread this as he was of the undead now and almost no human action was capable of imperiling him. She, though, had to love this man, Eumann, ferociously to play such a game. Being love's fool might cost her dearly but she seemed either oblivious or unconcerned about the risk.

They came around one of the odd huts and she bent to its margin. He suddenly discerned where he was being taken. She lifted what had seemed a simple sodden patch of ground and it rose in her hand. She lifted this intentionally soiled and disguised lid. Upon descent down hewn out steps, he recognized what once must have been a secret storage compartment. He was not able to conjure up any other reason for the existence of this elaborate underground site. But it was so wise! This obviously was a means of survival in war if all seemed lost. Yet it also seemed completely forgotten as well.

And it was to be his den; the perfect shelter for him as shield from the torment of sunrise.

CHAPTER 3

It Was To Be

Eumann was not surprised that the earthen interior had been well dealt with. The prior Eumann had his own skills and, with Catrione's aid, had shaped this area to that which was more habitable.

Catrione, once on flat surface, removed the already placed, slowly burning lamp at entrance foot. She needed this; he did not but pretended otherwise.

Along the hard packed walls, rectangular dirt indentations were filled with unlit oil lamps, one apiece. She set those she required aflame. Heat was generated and warmed the frigid spaces.

He saw the effort that had originally been expended in creating the passage to make it sufficient for short-term relocation of individuals and the storage of rapidly spoiled food in spite of its salting. In other words, the first builders had intended for it to be nothing but a long underground cut and hole through the dirt. Any stay of duration was to end in death as amenities were none.

He was pleased by the several refinements that the pair had brought to bear on the plain tunnel. Recollections were returning in fits and starts but returning they were. They had scraped out the indentations for the stone lamps. They had taken time and some patience to have dug out a convex area that served as bedroom for their coupling. The soil removed had been stomped into the flooring up passage. Straw had been laid neatly and thoroughly in this nook of theirs. The overall effect was elementary but was to suffice in passion's impatience. Their love did not demand softness, finery or subtleties. It was a yearning that cared not except for their urgent need to wrap arms around one another, whisper sincere sentiments into each other's ears, moan out their mutual desires and feel the infinite permutations of their flesh upon the other.

She withdrew a folded flaxen cloth from a corner of the room and spread it delicately over the ample straw heaped before them. She turned to him immediately after.

He approached her lovingly, softly. He truly sought her. This was no pretense on his part. And this was being yet ignorant of her nude shape. Her essence drew him to her without a shade of hesitation. He came to her and touched the brooch. Its workmanship was superb but cold with contact. Cold was not of his present sentiment and he unclasped it from just above her chest. The coupled rings that formed a chain linking itself to each side of the brooch he carefully unwound from around her neck. Her cloak was parted now with ease. She had used no belt around her waist. She had dressed for his easier access to her.

His pounding heart was glad to lay down these items and find the heat within the layers that she wore. Her long, pristine white tunic did not hold tightly to her body and so he remained uninformed as to her form. Beauty of face and spirit was enough he was realizing with her.

He sought out her skin and hoped for the same sleekness below the tunic as he felt upon her face. He traced her eyebrows with deft but very eager finger. He performed the same over her hot full lips. He craved removal of that tunic but let the burn of anticipation swell.

She did as prior and fondled his cock beneath his wool and knew of its arousal therefore. His arousal brought her arousal, the burn for the other rising rapidly and ecstatically.

She lingered at his cock an instant more and then stepped back from the intensive and tingling feel of his finger upon her. She cupped her palms over the thrust of both nipples against the tunic. He was planted and paralyzed with thudding pleasure as he witnessed her undulations.

She dipped her hands to mid-tunic and pulled leisurely up and out on the garment. This revealed her fuller nipples as they lengthened from the momentary self-stimulation. She continued to sway for him as she exposed her flattened belly. His cock firmed into very hard tube as she did this. She then bared the lower arch of her alabaster colored breasts. She held his gaze as she performed for him. His respirations were becoming labored and he had to have her very soon.

Upon finally exposing her chest to him, he comprehended that, yes, it was to be!

She extended her arms upward as she fully peeled the tunic from her and dropped it without regard onto the ground.

He was smote with the deliverance of his wish. She was exquisite. Her full mounded chest was gorgeous beyond any expectations or fantasies that lingered before. The tattoos emblazoned upon her body were nowhere near her breasts. That would have spoiled her natural gifts that projected toward him.

She did not blue herself as many Pictish women did.

He went to her immediately and she stood without a sound. The warmth of the lamps was swarming over them as he bent before her and suckled fiercely on one large caramel nipple and then the other. He licked with his tongue over each of her firming tips. She had her fingers entangled in his long chestnut hair but briefly. She quickly undid her braid, shook her head, and raked her fingernails over his back as he supped upon her thick nipples. He mixed his taste of her with quick and gentle twisting of each as well.

Her silence was broken. She moaned out this, "My love, lie for me. I must have that now." She tugged at his tunic and together they lifted it over his outstretched arms.

He maneuvered himself onto the bed, supine, as she then knelt over him. She permitted her very pendulous breasts to rock over his nipples. Then she took one of those breasts and rubbed it over his hirsute upper torso. Nipple tip to nipple tip was the most delicious though and she brought herself there again.

She dined at his nipples too. He was incredibly stimulated by this. His nipples were every bit as sensitive as hers. Her ministrations at his chest generated a swelling in his organ that was so erotic. It made his pulse throb there with an ache that he was hardly able to contain for want of release.

Catrione was in sexual turmoil for him as much as he for her. She hovered over his high standing shaft and took his flared cockhead into her mouth. His prominent vein at lateral surface of his thick and long member was cobalt and pulsing heavily. She took most of his engorged prod into her mouth to her throat and, with a hand locked around his length, pumped him up and down. She moaned and gasped for draughts of air intermittently. He groaned out his delight.

He commanded her to slide over his cock with her wetted and almost dripping sex. He had to experience her opening envelop him to his hilt. She did as he directed and sank down upon him and moaned at the stroke. She raised and lowered her hips upon his outsized cock and begged him to come as she neared her climax.

He felt his surge at the ready. So, when her waves tumbled from her and she cried out in bliss, he shot sprays that painted her inner vault thoroughly.

Their mutual release held for long moments together and then she leaned into his neck and kissed him over and over.

CHAPTER 4

A Lad Divided

Catrione had departed hours ago in a flurry of sighs and sorrowful words of temporary parting. Her anxiety to cover her absence and return to her usual bed was definitely paramount to them both. Once high emotion and lust had been sated, Catrione and Eumann relapsed into their grave concern of being in compromise over their clandestine and forbidden embrace.

His vision did not flow past the fact of her safe and unchallenged reappearance to her own chambers. His frustration at his vision's present limitations brought him to agonized concern for her. Basically, he had no choice other than to protect her regardless of the possible eruptions that could very well rear up suddenly.

He simply remained the day through in the more recessed bore that the tunnel provided. He required freedom from natural daylight with the earth comforting his backside at a minimum. These circumstances provided lean accommodations yet it was adequate. And that is how and where his subsequent twelve hours were spent and were always to be the same until he became other than Eumann.

Eumann awoke with one instinct pervading all others. And that was his profound sense of the divide branded

16

within and upon his pupil, the lad Cinaed. There was a quality to this boy that was much beyond the normal. His future seemed very bright to Eumann were he to survive all of the battling and warring amongst the hostile clans for territory and authority.

The singular concern resonating through Eumann's skull and sometimes responsive heart was that Cinaed had a notion of his and his mother's treachery regarding his beloved father. To Cinaed, Alpin was fearless, brave and all that he could seek in a parent. Eumann was also aware that Cinaed had a growing resentment of his teacher and his mother for this. It strained the child's capacity to take his mother seriously and Eumann's lessons with anything other than rebellion. Thus Cinaed ever waxed toward his father of majority Gaelic blood and waned toward his Pictish mother.

For his part, Eumann was presently helpless to perform differently. His impulses compelled him to engage in actions unwise but so overriding in passionate energy. Even for the boy, Eumann was incapable of stemming his and Catrione's tide. It was not extinguishable as its inevitability drove them forward into one another's arms.

He was also to explain to the boy, and for that matter the entire enclave gradually, the reasons for his attendance in their company only as the glowing yellow orb set and then only until it rose again. He was assured of his success there but was a bit cloudy on exactly his explanation. Ahhh yes, easy that! He would convince all that he had new pupils outside this encampment to teach during the day and was powerless to assist Cinaed during those hours.

So much deceit and bowing to helplessness in order to accommodate humans. He hated this. But he was prepared as he emerged from the tunnel and strode toward the wheelhouse neighboring the shelter where he had possessed Eumann originally. That was his purpose and Cinaed was awaiting him there.

Just prior to reaching the entrance to Alpin, Catrione and Cinaed's abode, a commotion ensued where the child and his mother bolted outdoors. They had heard the distant sounds before he had; probably Cinaed as he flew from the wheelhouse first. The boy had acute hearing and quite likely so much more. Eumann ran with them so as to give succor to or applaud the battle weary hoard that was slowly approaching them.

Many of these Dal Riatan soldiers were hoisting their swords in grand salute to their victory and their leader. A few sang but sang so tiredly and even fewer assisted their wounded compatriots. The ground trembled slightly with the footfalls of the massed and generally buoyant crowd.

Just rearward of the first line of men was an occasionally stumbling segment of closely guarded very humbled prisoners. Dal Riatan soldiers were notorious for only bringing home relatively healthy opponents. All other of these adversaries were lanced immediately and dispatched to their maker without mercy. This though was less savage than the Pictish who brandished hacked off heads aloft for all to see as their bloody souvenirs and grotesque symbols of their ferocity.

Cinaed clutched at his father's waist as all moved towards the community's core. Alpin kissed his son briefly on crown of his head and then, fearing inadvertent harm coming to his son in this mostly celebrating melee, brushed Cinaed away and pointed him to his mother.

Cinaed obeyed but did so grudgingly. Eumann was cognizant that the boy had confidence and was displeased that his father displayed any concern for him whatsoever.

Cinaed believed that he was well capable of taking care of himself; even among his father's troops. But his father was oblivious to the exceptional individual that Cinaed was and was to become.

In an effort to demonstrate to Alpin his proficiencies, Cinaed whirled around and scoured the brush and stone for any item to use for posing and poking. He crouched to the coarse terrain and grasped a short broken branch. He rose back up and did a child's version of a thrust and parry at one of the passing prisoners. He did not actually jab the dastardly individual but performed a genuinely menacing imitation of an adult soldier lashing out with his short spear. He repeated this tack over and over, ever hopeful that his preoccupied father would detect Cinaed's stabs. Catrione was the one though who observed Cinaed's eagerly aggressive prods and she reacted by pulling him out of harm's way. Cinaed glared at her viciously when she did this.

Alpin glanced in the direction of Catrione and reacted not at all. As was the custom of high ranking individuals, husbands were accorded permission to treat their wives with huge latitude. So, to Alpin, Catrione was no more than his possession; a creature to do his bidding. He owed her no affection and would show her none. Her allegiance and duty was to him and him alone. And besides, he smirked; she was of an alien tribe. She had been lucky that he spared her and had rendered her his wife.

Count your blessings Catrione!

The soldiers did not venture into battle with chariots or were they burdened with the weight of awkward armor. Some rode astride their prized horses. Some carried swords, small knives, and short spears; they might wear helmets and carry a rare shield. They all had their bare chests, their short trousers, their frightening battle tattoos, their sometimes spiked central patch of blond lye bleached hair and their demonic screams when attacking. This conviction of their superiority terrified most.

Eumann peered in Catrione's direction and gave her the tender look that had been void as an offering from Alpin to her, now or ever. The ledge of Catrione's vividly long dark lashes pointed his way and her sparking brilliant eyes beamed at Eumann though she did not move a facial muscle to smile or give secrets away.

CHAPTER 5

Her Tattoos

Alpin's return to hearth and home thrilled Cinaed to the utmost. He relished performing skills in swordsmanship, wrestling and heaving of the short spear, taught to him by Eumann, in Alpin's presence. Alpin treasured his son's enthusiasm and precocious abilities in close at hand combat. He was somewhat rough at larger strategic dynamics but, after all, he was a mere seven years old. Alpin, since his troop's earlier conquest of a portion of the decimated Strathclyde's, leveled concentrated attention upon Cinaed. Alpin even shared his zythos with his son. This fermented mixture of mead and barley managed to solidify their bond if not always their consciousness.

For that very reason, Catrione served her husband large draughts of the caramel colored brew on those opportune occasions when she and Eumann were unable to contain their mutual need for one another an instant longer. She hated the effect of the alcohol on Cinaed though. Both males ignored her wishes regardless and served themselves if she did not serve them.

All of this Eumann comprehended as he applied his psychic powers to whatever significant detail appeared. As he practiced and those powers of his smoothed and strengthened, his patience and calmness followed suit.

21

Eumann sighed at the fact that the undead, even one as ancient as he was, had distinct limitations and lessons to learn. Why had he not been created whole at his birth?

He pictured the boy and the man thoroughly drunk and pitched onto their straw beds snoring in fits and grunts; not enough to rouse them though. They were completely oblivious to all that surrounded them in their stupor.

Eumann anticipated Catrione's appearance as Alpin and Cinaed were never going to notice her departure this eve. He lay awake and restless in his excitement over her imminent presence. His cock stirred easily as well. She provoked his yearnings as if they were set to snap anytime. His blood was filling contracted vessels and flesh that were to swell much outsized soon.

From a distance, Eumann heard the disguised wood lid close and his breathing accelerated as she stepped in his direction. He had insured her ease of progress within the shaft by having already lit lamps and permitted that heat to penetrate the soil and always slightly humid, mildly smoky underground air. The humidity and flame joined to accentuate the warmth within. It was never ideal but it was what they had.

Catrione, having tasted a swallow of the barley and honey-mead concoction earlier, was relaxed and joyous. Eumann evinced this instantly as the illumination of lamp's flame coincidentally framed Catrione's face in fire; or what seemed like fire. Her beautifully aesthetic features were highlighted and that is how he so simply read her delight as she approached him.

He was standing, waiting and met her as she met him. Their embrace was so urgent that Catrione still carefully held the oil lamp at his mid back. Their lips pressed almost desperately together. Then she released from their clasp of

22

arms and lips and laid the lamp on its much more secure ledge.

She did not divest herself of her brooch and clothing slowly this time. She was in wanton desire for him and fled her attire quickly therefore.

His cock ached and flared as he peered at her wondrous nude figure. But he was almost uniformly as entranced with the tattoo markings present upon her supple skin. And so he reduced her rush and sat her down next to him on their makeshift bed.

"You are so golden, my love." This as Eumann ran his finger along her slightly parted lips. He was compelled to do this with her each and every time that they rendezvoused like this. Her lips were soft, warm, revealing, one area endearingly uplifted when she smiled and were one of the tender paths to her soul. Her lips and her eyes never failed to be her first magnets that drew him in.

He now steadied himself for a second and said this to Catrione as his fingers lingered in a flowing brush stroke to her cheek. "Tell me how you managed such an intricately done tiny tattoo here; and identically on your other as well. They are a perfect match. What skill that reveals. Were you the brilliant artist?"

"You have your own tattoos," Catrione spoke in hushed and breathless tones in her suppressed excitement for the union that she craved but put off to reply to his curiosity.

"But they are large and clumsy. They are good for masculine bravado but they do not compare to the finesse of yours. The tattoos you reveal to me, and you have revealed all my love, heighten your already stunning attractiveness."

"Yes, my love, I directed what and where but did not instill the butterfly designs into my skin myself. I must convey to you that I feel well protected by my tattoos. Yet you, my handsome Eumann, protect me the most."

With that uttered, she again embraced him and her lips clung to his.

Before his intellect escaped him, he instantly reviewed the tattoos upon her that stunned him in their ability to heighten, not only her exquisite form and look, but fashioned a uniqueness that pounded his senses into a whimpering longing for her. He was astounded at the intensive play of emotions upon his core that she generated for him. This was less than within his control and it pricked and disturbed him occasionally. But he knew not how to shake it from his gut, his loins, his usually stone heart. Baffling but he yielded to her call as it was so delicious. And these tattoos were part of that siren sound for him.

The blue of all her tattoo's vividly contrasted with her gently pale beckoning skin. She had the small design of a horse-like creature at her belly and it most especially undulated momentarily as he entered her. Above her ribs right and left were the watery shapes of fish. Her thighs and shins were decorated with miniscule circles with tails at distal end that might have been intended as the most delicate of snake or serpent. Below her nape was a horned head of a bull that, he guessed, was the ultimate tattooed source of protection for her. That one was fine as all the rest but had to have been done by another. There were designs of fragile flowers above her chest in an interconnected half circle exactly where the copper choker's links hung in their splendor. She had intended that effect assuredly.

It was a palate of single color that compelled him immensely.

And all this was from the common woad.

He was prepared to ravish her now.

CHAPTER 6

Smoky Love

Her charged embrace and lips that barely fell upon his own lips now, with hot, gentle waves of her excited breath, startled him out of all conscious thought and brought him to collapse into surging synapses, blood's engorgement and arousal manifest. Except to linger over them with loving caress, tattoos imploded and winked out of his brain.

Horizontal smoky wisps hung seductively and gracefully in the room, poised as Eumann and Catrione were poised in one another's arms. The stillness became prelude to an imminent uncoiling of potent emotion.

In this pause of anticipation, Eumann let his teeth graze her neck at her palpable throb. She moaned as the tiny ooze of blood that pinched from her delicately lacerated skin almost goaded him on. The ancient lust in him hissed tremulously on the brink of burying itself into buttery soft and creamy smooth flesh. The impulse nearly bettered him. He perceived that her unbridled urge showed no caution here; rent flesh or no. Her body yearned for his deeper prick and slash that would inevitably scorch her soul. The cost was no matter even if it were her undoing. And it would be unless he turned her. He had not felt this before but was loath to do that without her consent. He was edging toward a baffling empathy. He had found himself at a tipping point like this never before; to feed upon his heart's desire or to pull back from that precipice with her.

His undead core had mastered provoking this yearning in the fragile human spirit long ago. He was deeply mindful that passion's dominance, even when overarching release was only briefly experienced, compelled consummation of the siren call of those erotic needs. Yet, he required her soul, not her blood. And so, after he licked at the crimson droplets, he then passed on to the delights of hers that always transfixed him and compelled him to her.

Her body lost all tautness in her swoon at the touch of his fangs to her carotid. She pitched more severely into his surrounding arms as he caught that forward lurch of hers. He then fluidly supported her back with one arm and cradled beneath her limp and flexed legs with his other arm, then spread her upon the flaxen bed surface longwise. He observed her while she opened her eyelids and then she reached to stroke his chest.

It took seconds for her to flush and totally regain her color.

Her need for him combined with the blood urge was that intense for her. He was astounded and his bond to her crested so high. She was splendid in all ways; such potent physical beauty, a voluptuous and high kindled heat and an encompassing essence that choose to encourage and elevate.

He was enthralled as she leaned upward to him. Then she crouched over his straining clothing and slid the wool covering to the side. She grasped at the filling form of his manhood. She followed by dipping her tongue to his cock's tiny opening and tasted his clear drop that was produced when she slowly pumped and twisted his shaft. She trailed her remaining fingers over and between his thighs. She

26

permitted her fingernails to glide over his balls so subtly. She continued to pump his shaft up and down so that she was firmly milking more dew drops from him. Pumping still, her mouth encircled his cock, though she could only take half of it in. Her cheeks swelled as she sucked on him and attempted to swallow more of him. She gasped for air finally and returned to doing the same again. She pumped harder now and peered into his eyes. She no longer made contact with his sack and had both hands encircled at his thick organ. The side vein expanded bluish as she twisted the shaft and repeated that exquisite maneuver upon his cock. He underwent the barest of spasms and had to stop her immediately. He planned to come in another manner and was not ready yet.

He whispered in her ear, hardly able to rasp it out in his desire, "Get on all fours for me. Do that now my wonderful Catrione."

She did just that and then turned her head so that she witnessed his every action upon her. He lasciviously kissed her wondrous buttocks as if starving. Then he laid a finger upon that opening and simply rested his finger there for only seconds.

He grasped his instrument and placed his flared and throbbing cockhead into her wet cleft. She pushed back against him and whimpered at his entry into her Venus vault. He drew into her to her maximum and held still while he reached around to fondle her heavily pendulous and slightly swaying breasts. He cupped them to begin, using his large palms and long fingers to massage her orbs rhythmically. Then, cock remaining poised within her depths, he took her long and swollen brown nipples between thumb and forefinger and compressed her nipples repeatedly. He alternated with definite twists of those huge tips of hers.

She shivered in anticipation, paralyzed and gazing yet at him. She moaned then too with his ministrations to her nipples.

Then he began to thrust inside of her. He was definite in those thrusts and gained momentum rapidly. Her flesh around his thick member was a goad that melted his control. She alternated looking back at him and then whipping her head forward and downward; all the while crying in her heat. Her gorgeous mane was thrown back and forth, back and forth. She rocked into him as he plunged into her. He groaned and accelerated into her glistening folds.

That earlier spasm of his was tensing for not just an enlarged spasm but multifold large spasms. She cried, "Please, please, please" to him. He left her breasts and gripped her hips tightly. He hammered at her cherished insides then. She pumped into him hard but it was not enough. He made her do that harder as his grip rocked her harshly. He was unable to restrain himself longer. He lashed his huge spurts of come into her and it was this that blossomed for her into waves of delirious orgasm, the burn transformed. Catrione shook in the rigors of her ecstasy and Eumann had found his discharge huge.

She dropped to her belly and chest in exhaustion. He removed himself from her and fell beside her. His ejaculate seeped from her opening. It was love's elixir.

They slept entwined. When they roused, Eumann remained fascinated with Catrione's tattoos. Now it was not how expertly and artfully they had been done but how the dye had been so perfectly infused and the tattoos so wonderfully constructed.

Catrione smiled in a bemused fashion and tolerated his absorption once more. She was to explain the woad process thus, "If you are not already aware, I am an expert at the entire tattoo process. And I am skilled as obviously the tattooists for you were not. That is no insult as you are so handsome with or without yours.

Well now, I will be very specific. Interrupt me if you need to."

"I will not. But I will teach this to Cinaed." Eumann was bound by her and everything about her.

"The woad plant is the basis of my tattoos. Did you know that already?"

"I did know that and would guess they are the dye for my tattoos as well."

"They are.

To continue my love, the woad plant is cultivated, picked, crushed and then fermented. The entire process can take up to two years to accomplish. The crushed leaves are continuously tended to and these woad tenders pass their own water into the bowls holding the leaves. Then the finished leaves are dried into balls and pounded into the powder used for my tattoos, your tattoos, all that you see upon any body.

It is an imperfect process and that is why I am so valued. I have the ability to create consistent dye and can use my needles to tap the dye into the skin. I have designed so many tattoos and have also taught many the application processes as well.

You are the teacher but I am so happy to teach you also.

Are you satisfied?"

"I am well satisfied." And Eumann was.

They nestled together again, and he could not help but kiss her sweet lips and curvaceous breasts before they relaxed back into their silent glow and warm comfortable embrace.

CHAPTER 7

Manhood Upon Him

Masses of the involved inhabitants, and that was almost all able bodies, progressed toward Loch Fyne with oil lamps and torches held high in anticipation of the forthcoming event. This was a momentous occasion held under the impact of a moon unhindered by cloud or cosmic shadow of any kind. It was the first full moon following his fourteenth year; the year 825 A.D. It was the heathen method of inauguration; bringing a male individual into his prime. They were not wholly captive to Christianity yet. Columba had come and gone; Bede was the historian for that. Old customs and beliefs were intermingled and the old was breathing still.

This event glorified the coming of age, boy to man, of the righteous Cinaed, part royal Gael and part royal Pict. Thereby, he was to become an eventual force to be reckoned with. This was his moment of divestiture; he was about to put away his childish habits and dependencies as he reached toward a sense of himself as sure and strong, abilities of survival and care all encompassing.

He walked between two grey cloaked and hooded tall men. Third and fourth similarly dressed men trailed immediately behind. The two at his side and escorting Cinaed forward were the primary priest and Cinaed's father, Alpin. The two pacing in rhythm behind with the men and boy ahead were Cinaed's tutor, Eumann, and a secondary priest who moved in the stern seriousness that the ceremony merited.

They were soon to be at water's edge.

Eumann was unable to swivel his head and glance at Catrione who was in the next tier of people down. Her pride in the near ascension of her son into manhood vibrated around him and nearly drowned his psychic senses. In spite of the hidden discord between his mother and her son regarding her and Eumann's continuing rapture with one another, Catrione dismissed that kink between mother and son and demonstrated an almost drunk pleasure for Cinaed's upcoming test and ultimate triumph she was sure.

As the front line ceased, so did the remainder behind. Wavelets lapped calmly at the water's edge. Cinaed had been previously instructed by Eumann the step-by-step process through the ritual before him. Cinaed had treated his preparation for the celebrated event in the proper fashion. He had focused his attention on Eumann's demonstrations, had set aside what Eumann knew to be discord towards him in order to more precisely perform in return demonstrations to Eumann and he absorbed his lessons readily without overexcitement or foolish disregard interfering.

The principle priest took Cinaed's hand and both waded into the frigid liquid. As they did this, each row shifted a pace or two further so that all space to the embankment was filled. The priest guided Cinaed to water at the priest's knee height; for Cinaed, shorter than the druid before him, the water perched to and then slapped at Cinaed's mid thighs. The boy had nothing but a shortened set of trews on that were scarcely beyond the size of a loin cloth front and back. It was at this point that Cinaed copied a portion of Eumann's advice and stilled his mind, silently chanted an almost incomprehensible monosyllabic word and, thereby, hardly sensed the combined cold of air and water shooting frigid darts through his bluish skin.

The priest pointed at Cinaed and then swung his finger in a quick downward arch. Cinaed kneeled so that the Loch's surface washed over his chest and nipples. A small knife with dulled edges and a hilt that gave the instrument a cross-like appearance was drawn. At this gesture, Cinaed bowed his head and threw his arms wide at a ninety degree angle from his body. He was in absolute, though precariously balanced, supplication to his spiritual guide when that guide laid that shimmering blade upon his scalp and skull.

Cinaed felt the pressure as his head was slowly forced down under the water. Cinaed, whose passion did not include water skills except oaring a currach, nonetheless managed stone stillness all the while that his head was submerged. Eumann and he had definitely practiced Cinaed's underwater breath holding until Cinaed became fearless at it, blew no bubbles through his nose and froze without motion.

The blade lingered for a minute. Cinaed waited with lungs in beginning crisis. This was sensed and the blade relaxed upon him and then lifted so that Cinaed was able to raise his head in unison with the movement of the blade.

Upon resurfacing, Cinaed wanted to gasp. He was not permitted this. Only children and creatures less than men revealed their weakness in uncontrolled actions and behavior. Cinaed continued to quiet himself and let breath seep into his chest steadily and with grace.

"You have been superficially cleansed of boyish remnants. Turn now and face to the shore. Next, this newborn skin of yours shall be permanently marked."

In Pictish society, Cinaed's mother would have approached her as yet boy. And with her expertise, she would have become his first tattooist. But alas, this was Dal Riata and Gaelic. Patrilineal customs ruled and superseded the matrilineal customs of the Pictish. No female was allowed to make contact with Cinaed's virginal about-to-be adult skin. That was sacrilege!

So, as Cinaed strode out of the midnight glazed water, Alpin and the second priest strode toward Cinaed. They met mid-distance where Alpin then dried his son's skin thoroughly with a large flaxen cloth. Cinaed's flesh had to be bone dry for the ink to be successfully applied. In addition, Cinaed was cold as hell as well; but that aspect of the toweling off was ignored by all.

The priest whose cloak was water saturated at its bottom stepped into the shadows as the second priest set his oil lamp and working utensils and dye to the ground at Cinaed's feet. Others in the dense crowd were allowed to place their lamps surrounding Cinaed and the priest as well. In this manner, the delicate job of tattooing would be accomplished with more than adequate illumination.

Alpin took the slightly damp cloth and spread it over the thin sandy margin that lay proximate to Cinaed. Cinaed dropped to the cloth in a single agile burst and spread himself prone over the material. This druid had his own tiny knife with a wickedly sharpened blade. He sat cross-legged at Cinaed's side. He then rearranged the boy's long dark hair to the side; whereupon he laid the knife edge to the downy mass of hairs at neck nape and expertly shaved a rectangular area there.

Once done removing the hair, this priest started tapping woad blue dye into Cinaed's absorbent subcutaneous layers with a sharp-tipped, long handled and slender tool.

As time passed, and Cinaed was not permitted a sound or a stir from the pain, the shape of a huge red buck formed. The tattoo, of course, was not red in color but aggressively red in spirit. This was Cinaed's animal protector and would often see him to marvelous positive fortune.

CHAPTER 8

Righteous Buck

Below the righteous buck was tattooed the flaring sun at Cinaed's mid lower back.

A horned bull, much as Catrione wore at her nape, was newly inked above his already muscled pectorals. This was but one of many that the deft priestly artist punctured into Cinaed's skin. The tattoos on his back had been completed hours before this achievement of the bull. The buck and the bull were to be Cinaed's pride evermore. And they had been inked as skillfully as Catrione would have accomplished; she, Alpin, Eumann, all were equally as fascinated by the human painted tapestry before them.

The leaves of the woad plant rose from his navel and fanned skyward in pursuit of Godly recognition. The druid tattooist had primitively done rude wavering fish at both of Cinaed's upper wrists. Rain drops were tatted to each proximal digit of his fingers. Tiny fanged and coiled snakes prepared to strike were placed at his smoothly mounded biceps. Miniature spears were softly mounted to the flesh of his inner thighs, one tip pointed downward and the other upward. Finally, a single wheeled star was embedded into that part of his body-palette that was his upper left foot. For now, until further accomplishments, his forehead and cheeks remained clear.

The shocking pain had repeated itself seemingly without end or mercy. Manhood was much less thrilling than Cinaed had anticipated. If this bit of torture were to whisper secrets into his ear of years to come, he was certain that those hushed intonations would tickle his mind with images of tribulation, hard challenges ahead and pain, oh so much pain!

Yet he had been well instructed by his very knowledgeable Eumann as to modes and methods of suppressing the torment; of morphing a black ball of sensation into miniscule size, sound and fury so that it would slip away into the deepest, most inaccessible folds of his mind. He comprehended that he was likely to endure almost any tempest that inevitably would grind into his endeavors were he to use that particular mental approach.

The shadows were running scared before the potent yellow round that was raising steadily, horizon bound. Eumann was ready to be away and protected. Yet he required himself, as did Cinaed's onlookers, to stay until Cinaed was off on his own into the stony and erratically timbered woods at their shoulders.

The priest sat upright then; on some level intuiting Eumann's necessity to soon depart. The last tattoo had been done hurriedly but, in spite of that, was well done. He then closed his eyes and swept his hands almost skimming Cinaed's skin surface. This sweep progressed from midpoint to head with one hand and midpoint to toes with the other hand. Even though his vision was nonexistent, he made absolutely no contact with Cinaed whatsoever.

It was obvious that the druid's legs ached from hours locked in a single posture but after his arms passed over Cinaed's body, he stood to his full height without difficulty and opened his eyes to peer down at his work. Cinaed remained supine and fixed.

The priest spoke, "Arise now my child. You are, as yet, a child. If you overcome a final test, you will never again be called child."

Cinaed rose up off of the flax as gracefully as had the priest. He faced the crowd before him and then did not shift his stance whatsoever. He gazed off into the distance. Eumann comprehended that this gaze was Cinaed girding himself for the test's travail.

The priest reached beneath his cloak to once again reveal the tool that had been wielded so delicately to shave Cinaed's hair.

"Take this and use it as your sole weapon. You have two cycles of the moon to present to us a wild cat killed only with this.

If you accomplish this, you will have our infinite respect that you are well ready to take your station amongst men. If you fail, you will be disregarded and considered child until your next birthday when you will attempt the hunt again."

Cinaed was handed the small blade.

"You begin this test immediately. Go now and find the one cat that will be sacrificed by you so that you may carry forth in honor."

The human mass parted once these words had been uttered. Cinaed scrambled to the woods.

To find himself independent and free of the anguish of the demanded paralysis of the ritual infused him with a burst of energy that was short lived. So much of his energy had already been used and abused. But that was the reason that this ceremony had been employed for ages. It was harsh and separated the weak from the strong. For those who might one day become rulers, it was absurdly challenging as the

European Wildcat was ferocious and clever. Most fourteen year olds were given much meeker beasts to slay. The clan lay their hopes at Cinaed's feet and they were not about to trust one unworthy and incapable.

Eumann fled to his shelter; the very same shelter that he and Catrione had carefully never forfeited.

As the vampire settled into his seven year make shift coffin at the bowels of the supply tunnel, he was astonished to realize that his once voraciously cruel heart was being kneaded and presently yielded to all fashion of puny and even sometimes sensitive emotions. He had granted no reprieve to any that had begged his tolerance or forgiveness pastime.

Now he considered two of those very unpalatable notions, one prior and one current. When he arrived in this circle of common inhabitants, he had almost reflexively chosen to feed outside of the walls of the city. Dal Riata was safe from his undead ravages. The other was immediately concerning and was this: he had to help Cinaed for the boy to survive. And he would do exactly that as the sun vanished.

His last image before he took his obligatory sleep was that Cinaed was already fatigued and stumbling loudly through branches that he scarcely brushed aside.

CHAPTER 9

Thin Wire

Ascent from the slumber at daylight's finale gained momentum until Eumann was a blur of activity. He had rescue motivating his flight from the soiled chamber, out the single known exit, and then sending himself upward simultaneous with his instant reconfiguration into loathed shape. The hiss of the wind beneath his webbed wings lofted him more quickly and gave further drive to his acceleration.

He and Cinaed had exerted themselves in the practice of Cinaed's identification, then identification again, of edible plants in the wild. How much of this had the boy retained? And there was also a vast difference between ability to successfully search out what had just been taught in comfortable surroundings versus the same under the duress of circumstances where one's life was balancing on a thin and breaking wire. Had Cinaed remembered the flora to use for body disguise if need be? That would greatly serve him in his approach to the cat. And how much had the exhaustion of the rigorous ritual before foot even anticipated forest's maw weakened him? The burn of his fresh tattoos and the energy consumed for that healing drained strength and diminished concentration for anything else except to pass through to a painless state.

The bat was in grave fear in regards to Cinaed; and, though he was of advanced skills and power for his age, the fact that he was fourteen screamed out at the flying form. In their overzealousness for proof of ability, the vampire had easily discerned that the clan had seriously misjudged and put their own best opportunity for future advancement in high jeopardy. This test was beyond Cinaed's capacity to do.

Yet Eumann had been powerless to assist in the last twelve hours. Now he was in terror that he was too late. Cinaed was so crucial to the formation of history and he must not die! His psychic sense did not tell him this; his instincts did.

From the sky's vantage point, psychic powers honed to a sharp point and with eyes of the undead, the creature sighted Cinaed. He shot as if he was the rock of a slingshot and streaked to his furred target.

His fangs were straight and true as they lanced forcefully into sinewy flesh. The thing howled and helplessly continued its midair leap from the precipice.

The craggy low lying precipice hovered above Cinaed. In his frail, famished, exhausted and near hypothermic condition, he just sensed his danger but was beyond parsing out the details of his imminent peril. His legs trembled in rushes beyond his control, he panted in the sharp piercing pain of frigid cold combined with having run dumbstruck through the day. Now it was night and soon to have temperature's descent cripple him even further. His gut rumbled in defiant sounds of starvation. Dehydration pinged through his physiologic system as well. This caused him additional faintness and vision loss that was about to reduce him to blindness.

All that he managed was to hold his sorry small knife in his numbed and shivering hand. All sounds caused him to jerk around and slash at imaginary enemies. He had no hope and knew that he was about to die.

The following sound was not false. Cinaed spun in its direction as best as he could and held his single weapon aloft.

The impact of the snarling, then crying wildcat, glanced off his side, knocked the blade out of his grasp and into the brush. He staggered from the animal's leap that had, for some inexplicable reason, veered from him and did not crush him as would have been had full impact occurred. If that, the cat would have supped on him without interference or struggle from Cinaed.

As it was, Cinaed was hurled to the uneven rocky surface, fell into unconsciousness and was still. He had seen nothing, felt everything and now was silent.

The vampire had taken a gamble that he could lay the cat low before Cinaed was killed. He also took the further risk that Cinaed would not observe him riding the throat of the cat in the cat's arch toward Cinaed. He had probed into Cinaed's temporary blank mind and discerned that Cinaed had observed virtually nothing in his weakness, surprise and certainty of his own death. This potential hazard was taken because the undead fiend was so enamored of Catrione that he was not about to sacrifice the connection in order to inhabit Cinaed and use that means to conquer the cat.

No, he was desirous of remaining Eumann as he so defenselessly loved being in Catrione's arms; and he was able to save Cinaed without radical transformation on his part. So instead he had held back fractionally.

The wildcat dropped to the forest surface and was mangled from its rent throat and fractured bones. The cat had taken its last breath and bled copiously.

The blade was discovered in a shallow stone crevice and Eumann, in human form again, shoved it to its hilt into the pierced area of the cat's shredded throat. The handle would shine when Cinaed awoke.

Eumann drifted back into the deep gloom and remained to observe and protect the downed boy. Upon his assurance of Cinaed's success, he would fly back to the village unnoticed, take on his human form once again and never be revealed as the true slayer of the cat.

Cinaed's eyelids fluttered, he gazed out of focus momentarily. He gasped as he realized that he had survived. How could this be? He had been so dazed and such easy prey. Yet there was his blade shoved deep into the cat's gaping hole between head and body!

He rejoiced. There was only one possible explanation for the fact that life and breath yet resided in him. The animal must have landed on the blade and it pierced the cat's jugular fatally.

Cinaed sat, prayed to primitive Gods, gathered his wits then and struggled, in time, to bring the carcass to the priests.

He was rendered man upon their immediate recognition of what would become a storied deed.

He had to endure one more intervention before he was permitted to leave the ceremonial area. There were almost no spectators for this as many had returned to their daily duties after so much passing time. Only significant relations and favorably regarded associates remained.

The priest tattooist performed diligently and industriously. He placed the two symbols in spite of his grasp of Cinaed's need for food, water and rest.

Those tattoos were burned in woad blue over his temples and curved in frightening form below and above his eyes and spilled ferociously onto his cheeks and forehead additionally.

They meant strength; the strength of the one indomitable Cinaed.

CHAPTER 10

Pictish Choker

Eumann's limited foresight brought him this knowledge at least.

Her bulky silver choker was stunning but its weight never left her mind. It had been a present given to her on her sixteenth birthday by one of her adorable friends. This constant companion of hers, also of a wealthy family, had lineage that was Pictish. It was rare in Dal Riata but did occur. And this gift had been crafted carefully by Pictish hands. This friend loved Aiobheean so and had impulsively presented it to her for it to be worn in honor of their connection.

The intent was there but Aiobheean did not wear it upon her neck evermore, as it turned out.

Much of her early youth, and she was now twenty one years old, had been as a sheltered young girl and then blossoming adolescent. She had been treated this way because of her high borne parents. Her parents loved her well. They also knew her value in joining with an exceptional royal male. These parents may have even gone to an extreme. They had kept her within the confines of their vast wheelhouse those twenty one years. They had also insulated her from mingling socially only with, when she was permitted to mingle at all amongst other than family, females of well to do lineage.

Aiobheean had appreciated the protection as she had appreciated her parents. It was a harsh world she indirectly perceived. She was willing to sample exposed life but only as she was prepared for that. And she was that now.

Energy for broader experience vibrated through her. Her loins felt the excitement too as every time she fantasized upon the male form, none in particular presently, all in the general, a throb began to buzz within her. This force started at her neck, beneath her very choker, swiftly descended to her thickening, lengthening nipples, to shining, smooth and reddened clitoris and ultimately lodged in her moist and lubricated vault. She was most assuredly set to find her larger experience.

At this age, finally, Aiobheean was no longer under such strict scrutiny. Tradition dictated that at the turn of a daughter's twenty first year a father had to release her to the larger world. At first, early in that year, she had been escorted by a family elder. It was preferred that this was the way always but Aiobheean had a bit of a demanding nature here and now. She wanted no escort whatsoever; at least oft times. Her family yielded to her insistence upon this but bade her go short distances from home when walking alone. She agreed. She was full of appetite for life but she was not careless or unwise.

She wandered therefore on her own occasionally as her prior escorts had familiarized her with the close at hand areas of her own city. She always stayed close enough but bravely sought new pieces of neighboring territory on her sojourns.

Aiobheean meant beautiful fair form in the Dal Riatan language. And this young woman was more than worthy of this especial name. She had so many of those magnificent qualities that were often bequeathed to the Dal Riatans. But her beauty transcended even their beautiful norm. She had long strawberry blond hair with a fine sheen and luster to her soft curls. She had such silken skin that it was almost sensuously aching to lay fingers upon it. Its wonder was alabaster-like in its creamy regularity and tender feel. Her pinched rosy cheeks offset the porcelain surface of her face so magnificently that the few freckles that danced on her nose and cheeks were hardly noticeable. And when they were seen, they were held in awe as well. The eyes washed over others so gently in an aquamarine blue with flecks of emerald green and gold. In the midst of this radiance was a set of full lips stained in a lush raspberry color. Rapture upon laying eyes to this wondrous being.

Her tunic that she wore frequently was unable to hide the exquisitely full and round mounds that proudly thrust themselves forward. Her very ample size did not cause them to be pendulous. They would be as she aged but they would be ever beautiful. Through the material, where her nipples pressed, one knew that her gorgeous flesh there was upturned and of the same raspberry stain as her innocent, yet incredibly enticing, lips. Her belly had the tiniest bit of roundness; that feature was so very feminine. Finally, her legs were lean and supple. She was pleased at their contour and softly muscled tone.

It was one of those brilliant but deeply chilled days where the cloudless azure sky brought all light but no warmth. Aiobheean was restless and primed for a stroll of her own this day. She draped her cloak over her body but did not place the hood upon her head. She bounded for the door and departed without any escort at all.

The roughness of the pathways and rudimentary streets remained somewhat alien to her. Or maybe it was not so much that as her home had its definite coarseness; maybe it was more so the swirl of activity amongst the bodies of a rather large population. Her prior isolation had unnerved her somewhat as she gathered amongst unruly crowds.

Equally as difficult for her was the attention that she garnered wherever she went. Heads turned, curious and lusting eyes stared, hushed words fell from the mouths of the citizenry, there were even uncouth exclamations from louts or drunks. Typically, when confronted with the swing and sway of many active people together, nearly shoulder to shoulder in the cramped quarters, she turned and fled back to her sanctuary. Today though was not that day. She was determined to shove past her fear and explore minutely further.

She had only ventured to Loch Fyne once that she recalled. That is where she would go today. It was near enough for safety's sake but far enough to satisfy her desire for adventure. She swiftly parted the crowd and strode to the water's edge. It took her but minutes as it was within view of the city center.

Upon planting her covered feet on the lean strip of giving white sand at the perimeter of the Loch, she removed the leather from those feet. She was eager to feel the sensations that the tiny grains of sand were to bring her. She was so new to the impression that it almost tickled. The spurt of slightly wet and mucky sand between her toes fascinated her even as it disconcerted her a bit too.

She sat upon the sand then and enjoyed the give of the tiny grains under her taut buttocks. The stuff conformed to her shape perfectly. That amused her no end. Such innocence and delight in the clarity of the elemental.

Eumann saw Cinaed see. And what Cinaed saw was Aiobheean. He had followed her as only a stricken and suddenly enamored nineteen year old youth can do. He had no motivation other than his own pure impulse of an onslaught of attraction. His first and only view of her ever had occurred moments ago. He felt helpless and could do no other than step with her from many lengths behind.

He was fascinated in his view of her as she began to wash the sand off of her garments.

She turned and he was totally unprepared for the further assault upon his senses that her splendor inspired in him.

CHAPTER 11

As Am I

Eumann smiled. He was cognizant that his talent of sinking into other's intimate spaces was improving rapidly. The subjects in Dal Riata had so much to offer him to practice on.

Aiobheean's unexpected pirouette slayed Cinaed as if a healthy European wildcat had leapt from a rocky ledge upon him and clawed his life away; admittedly, the pain was a trifle more pleasant in his present situation. He was stunned, paralyzed, enamored, confused and forever hers. She on the other hand lost not a beat as she gently chastised Cinaed. "I glimpsed you prior and let you follow.

You are filthy!

And, I am aware of who you are."

She let fly a sweet laugh then and asked, "Have you not bathed then?"

The emotional tone between the two, that positive kinetic force that was immediately palpable, their bound destiny as well, hummed hugely in this charged instant. It was as if he was an automaton and approached her with gaze riveted to hers. He spoke no words. His tongue was tied in such a Gordian Knot that freeing it seemed impossible.

He slowly legged past her, eyes still locked upon hers, turned and backward stepped into the icy blue water. The frigid tentacles that would ordinarily have left him gasping were not noticed whatsoever. He had been transfixed and was to stay in that trance as it brooked no alternatives. He began to flail and splash at the water in a weak, almost nonexistent, effort at cleansing himself.

Aiobheean glittered in delight at this captive demonstration of his. His tattoos mesmerized her thoroughly. She most especially observed his fierce buck and dark blue sun spanning his backside. The gravity and strength of these designs upon him made her feel a concentrated heat and beginning burn between her legs.

Her heart palpitated apace as she observed him toss water onto himself haphazardly. It had been at her suggestion and that pleased her much. She was easily as enraptured with him as he was entranced by her.

She welcomed the wetness that built and spread between her legs and glazed itself at her inner thighs. It was enticing that he was high borne as she was; more so actually. But it was what she viewed that caused her vault to allow her juices to start and advance.

Her vision was this. He had a braid of lengthy dark, auburn hair. His facial hair was in late adolescent patches of softness, but it was apparent and growing toward a decent fullness. There was to be prominent beard and hanging scimitar-like mustache in his entirely adult prime. The facial hairs wildness was almost comical in its feeble labors today. She, though, was very affected by this and it struck her as adorable.

His eyes, oh his eyes, were large in this moment and definitely told of a set that was a clear dark brown ale color with starbursts of cinnamon speckled throughout.

There was developing bulge at his biceps and triceps. Without thought, Aiobheean paced a few steps toward him.

She had let her cloak fall open long ago. The exposure of her tunic to him was unconsciously done and she was not alert to it at all. She felt an ache at her prominent nipples and wanted him to join his lips to them immediately.

He had courtesy enough enduring in his residual intelligent thoughts that had not yet departed to face away from her when he removed his short trews to sluice the grit and grime from his groin. He ducked under and then rose up in his efforts to cleanse himself there. He held his trews in one hand and quickly washed his genitals. Then, as he sensed that Aiobheean continued an intense stare in his direction, he wheeled around and let his manhood front her for an instant. Then he replaced his trews slowly.

His firmness had risen slightly just as he covered himself.

This beautiful Aiobheean had witnessed so much that she found more than exceptional; this was her man and he would be until the day that she died. That this came to her while regarding the prowess of his sexual organs had simply been coincidental. Her love and lust for Cinaed had been extant from his appearance at the city center. It was just that the strong bunched form of his buttocks coupled with the sight of his cock from posterior and anterior stance was the final thread that stitched her love and lust together in completed and permanent form.

She had nearly dashed into the lapping wavelets at the precise second that she saw how long and thick his cock was flaccid and cold. She had been able to view part of its wide dangle and bulbous cockhead from between his legs as his rear faced her. But then he had shown his tube to her in all of its wide, thick, long glory.

Oh how would it look upon its erection? She had had a taste of that momentarily as he redressed himself.

She was determined to discover his complete size at their first opportunity.

This was not that opportunity though.

They met perfectly at water's edge and she removed her cloak with which to dry him. She was brief in this and then threw the cloak back over herself. The frosty temperature was too much for her to bear for long.

He managed to remove his glance from her this time and peered down, then rolled the links of her choker between curious and excited fingers. The silver of it shone brightly and he was magnetized by its touch and appearance. He had never observed a larger or better crafted choker than this one was.

"I love how you wear this chain." Cinaed had conquered his Gordian knot at long last.

Aiobheean lifted her elegant and sleeved arms up to the clasp at her nape. She unclasped it carefully. "It is yours my handsome man. It is yours forever more. As am I."

CHAPTER 12

Shimmering Sparks

Aiobheean reached around Cinaed's neck and tried to clasp the choker. She needed his help to hold his long auburn hair up. At the back of Cinaed's neck was where their hands met; the very first intimate touch of skin.

The pledge of the choker made it all feel different now; the unwritten permission was granted to continue the journey in discovering and coming to know one another intimately. Once the choker was clasped, their hands joined together in front of them with fingers outstretched and palms touching. This was the first place to feel the syncopated breathing that was steadily quickening.

Their eyes locked reflexively. Starbursts and flecks were shimmering sparks as they gazed at the other. Aiobheean's cheeks were hot and blushing a deep shade of rose. Their fingers intertwined and their young bodies came even closer together still. Their lips nearly touched. Aiobheean's were swollen and pinched with the raspberry stain; Cinaed's spiced mocha in color with the bow so well defined.

But she had seen adults kiss. This first kiss as others' first kisses was no less awkward. Aiobheean and Cinaed smiled a little as they turned their faces right, left to the middle until they could finally meet in the moment of their first of oh so many of these pleasurable moments to follow.

Cinaed took Aiobheean's face in his hands and, as he kissed her lips so softly and gently, his thumbs brushed her flushed porcelain cheeks. His mustache tickled her as his kisses continued one after another. His eyes were closed, drinking it all in, but Aiobheean wanted to be open and aware of every nuance. She closed her blue eyes for an instant and then opened them quickly so that she was to feel and know every single second of this exquisite joy; mocha and raspberry lips lingering was the perfect combination of sweetness!

Cinaed's kisses multiplied as he found his arousal taking on a life of its own. Aiobheean put a finger to his lips to slow him down some. She liked lingering in the long slow kisses that brought more heat. Their lips soon parted and she let the very tip of her tongue peek between his lips. He immediately responded by taking that tip into his mouth and sucking on it. She felt this all the way down to her reddened and swollen cherry clit. He explored her mouth with his tongue and she in turn sucked the tip and right away felt his manhood respond.

Their hands moved from cheeks to necks. Oh, the choker felt heavy and wonderful around his neck.

Their fingers compared note as to what they were detecting and that was that Aiobheean's skin was so incredibly silky and feminine. Cinaed loved stroking it with the back of his hand.

Again he felt the stirring of his manhood. In the last several years, maybe more, Cinaed had awakened with a stirring feeling like this in his cock, but didn't understand what should or would come next to bring him relief and release. His fresh young cock was snaking up his belly, swelling and peeking out from his trews.

At the same time, his eyes were travelling from Aiobheean's face to the mounds on her chest, under that tunic. He lifted the cloak from her shoulders and let it fall to the ground just behind her. He was compelled to feel these mounds! And she, with his heat nearby, found the means to not only survive but to overcome the frigid air that she had been unable to bear just earlier.

Aiobheean felt her own stirrings and quickly loosened the tunic and lifted her arms to have Cinaed assist in its removal. Her nipples, hard as the pebbles that were now under their feet, darkened more into their berry color as they ached for his contact only. Aiobheean had touched herself before and reveled in the feeling that palming her own nipples brought her. She was aware that this caused her wetness to build and glisten in the bright red curly fur of her Mons. The warm and tingling sensation that this brought, created a need in her; a drive to have something fit just right inside her and fill her up. Aiobheean looked into Cinaed's eyes with her own, the emerald green flecks glowing in tiny bursts that danced, showing her want and her need.

Cinaed's hands moved to cup her breasts and his thumbs stroked over her nipples. When he fondled her, the softness contrasted with the hardness of her nipples, his cock jerked in response, and grew longer and thicker. He jumped with this sensation, as it took him further than he had ever been before. He moved his face lower and his lips so close that his downy mustache bristled slightly against her tender skin there. His lips opened and he took a nipple into his mouth and Aiobheean breathed in but not out. Her strawberry curls cascaded over his head and she moved them gently aside, so that she could watch him in his delight. She held his young face there and as he kissed and began to suckle, she felt her knees grow weak, and the sense of urgency that was now her own, build stronger. She had to have more of his love!

His cock was so long and thick now, straining against his trews, peeking up and out, the constriction adding to his engorgement. The first drops of his dew were forming at the tip. He yearned to be touched himself and shifted his hips toward Aiobheean to urge her on. She had no qualms about reaching out to grasp him. Tearing at the trews, she cast them aside. She squeezed this burgeoning cock and it flared out bulbous and reddish purple like a ripe plum! A patch of wiry auburn hair protected his sack. The dew drops were beginning to spill over. Aiobheean used her thumb to spread his liquid around, so his entire cockhead glistened.

As she did this, they both lowered to the ground, entwined. Instinctively they knew where this desire was leading them. Aiobheean lay upon her back and her body responded automatically by the raising of her knees and then opening wide. Between her legs, Cinaed found her center. Her curly red hair covered pink lips which easily separated to reveal her polished ruby clit. His own thumbs massaged gently there and her hips rose to meet him in a passion that silently told him, "Now!" His thumb found her moist opening, but met some resistance.

Aiobheean was gently moaning and panting, needing to feel Cinaed's throbbing cock inside her! He had to have her equally and they moved a little clumsily in their near desperation. He brought the dew kissed tip of his cock to her opening. She looked small and fragile there, and he was afraid that he might hurt her. Cinaed wanted to take his time but his desire told him to hurry! She elevated her hips to meet him and then began to guide his cock into her. Oh! the pain and pleasure in one! She cried out as his member passed through her maidenhead!

The initial pain gave way to the pleasure that they both had been seeking. Ohhhh! Cinaed's slick cock stroked in and out of Aiobheean's vault and it was not long before he began shooting his very first spurts of semen into her. His jets were hard and furious, lasting forever. Aiobheean responded with her own shivered moans of ecstasy! She threw her head back and cried out, raising her hips more to meet his rapid and forceful thrusts.

That they were thinly screened from view mattered not as they voiced their mutual joy.

From the top of her strawberry blonde head to the tip of her toes, as if many a rattle was vibrating over her skin and pulsating into her clitoris and lips in tiny bursts of thrill, she climaxed rhythmically, over and over, her muscles clenching and releasing deep inside her. Her vault clutched Cinaed's still hard cock throughout.

CHAPTER 13

Dark History

He leaned into the compact wall of soil that supported his spine and body as he sat cross-legged and fully awake, yet calm, in the shelter of the earth's embrace. Eumann had fed. Catrione was, per his sight, unfortunately wrapped in Alpin's arms as those two slept. At least one slept, loudly, with snorts gusting through his nose intermittently while the other wished for her own sleep or rather to be snuggled in with Eumann no matter the location. Eumann knew that she detested Alpin and all that he stood for; bravado, violence, maltreatment of women and, generally, his drunken ways. But sadly, she was his wife.

Cinaed was long unconscious as he had refused all lessons that night.

So Eumann was alone and had slaked his thirst only a few hours ago. He was content and permitted his mind to venture where it would, good or no. He was frightened of nothing, or so he believed. And this mental journey hastened him to both conjecture of and precise memories from his past times and prior habitations. His first was abundantly evil and that was as the hugely bullying and harsh tyrant Mezopx, son of Cain and Lilith.

He vaguely comprehended that he had had no body of his own even initially. Yet, corporeal or not, he had to draw blood to maintain his life. He simply did this invisibly when in between habitations. He guessed that he had been summoned by some divine, or evil, force to blossom into Lilith's belly from the seed of his father, the defiant and raging one who was Cain. And from his mother's loins, sprang the combination of vampire spirit blended with human form in the visage of the killer Mezopx; the unstoppable Mezopx.

Where the demon acquired the intangible energy that supported Mezopx's ghoulish character was unknown to Eumann, unknown to Septimius, even unknown to Mezopx, Lilith and Cain. God himself only discerned this. And was it a part of a heavenly plan to move all under His dominion in a particular direction? This God was not revealing His secrets to Eumann anytime but in the far bye and bye, if that, Eumann presumed.

His images drifted to his earliest days as Mezopx then; that period was certainly a slice of his very dark history. He had forever been attracted to water and the dry wasteland that oft surrounded bodies of water elsewhere. This was because his earliest memories were of youthful episodes cast upon the edges of the Tigris and Euphrates Rivers. It was profoundly ironic then that he was presently ensconced in a region that, yes, had water most certainly but none of the desert-like qualities of his boyhood. He was far afield from those climes here and now.

Thoughts percolating to and fro, Eumann returned to his incarnation as Mezopx. Though he had relished life in all its brutal basics then, in retrospect, he had matured some since. The simplicity of those ferocious warrior days had filled him up completely. In reconsideration, he was some sorrowful that he had conquered lands and enslaved many for, fundamentally, his greater glory! If in the process of wasting the enemy in that greater glory, a coincident positive happening occurred, so be it. But that was most assuredly a tiny aside for him then.

What he truly cherished eons ago was to charge down upon a terrorized foe in the various shades and darkness of sunless skies and butcher, behead and then feast upon these victims. Unlike his warrior brethren, who were not undead, he not only rejoiced in the death of others, but he lapped up their blood as well. No prisoners were ever kept when he led.

His battle charged armies cared not about this. They followed him anywhere and never rebuked him as he was the tyrant king and he always was victorious. He and his were Akkadians and they swept southward in perpetual advance. The Sumerians fell to Mezopx unending quest for blood; first, last and always. The weapons of the Sumerians were inferior and they were merely out slayed by Mezopx.

Eumann flinched a bit in replaying these past righteous moments of his.

He had a pause as he cast his thoughts to a question of his killing juggernaut. He was pinged with a sense of the barbarism of it all. That though passed almost instantly through him.

He had established a kingdom of city states; then recalled his transparent joy as the first emperor of his known world, probably the entire world. Even the Indian continent and the Chinese civilization were hardly developed yet. His capital, Akkad, became Babylon in later years.

Before his empire was brought to its knees by the city state of Ur, Eumann had been made to flee Mezopx body by instruction of his master. So, he was not able to pridefully take the credit for the initial advent of written language, use of the wheel, irrigation of crops nor the establishment of libraries himself.

That came after Mezopx.

Millennia eroded into his time since then and his recollection blurred as he counted the years out of body waiting for another body. He fed but was absolved of any shape or form. He felt as if he was a black spider who snatched at his prey and then waited eternally. It was an apt comparison except for the spider's corporeal nature and its web.

It had been two and a half millennia until he was granted human form again. This human that he inhabited at about two hundred years after Christ's birth, was a Roman bureaucrat who, again through vicious machinations, became an emperor. He was the eternal essence that seized human form and was named Lucius Septimius Severus.

Eumann realized that as Septimius, he had evolved only minutely from Mezopx. But he had evolved nonetheless. Eumann discerned the subtle reaching of a higher comfort at the knowledge that evil's progression might move toward deeper good rather than a movement toward a more mired evil.

How, though, had Septimius bettered Mezopx in that regard? Blood lust would always be present. So what prompted his mind to linger on these particulars of his history and the emotions of that history to drive his deeds? His heart was cast and cast in a cold shell, was it not? He wondered and was perplexed.

This thread of thought disturbed Eumann. But he found himself upon its path and was incapable of doing other than to follow it.

So how was he as Septimius gentler than his inhabited Mezopx? Eumann smiled wryly to himself. That took very little to manage as Mezopx was devoid of any goodness whatsoever. Septimius had connived, deceived, brought death to his perceived malefactors in the political halls in Rome that stamped rule upon the citizenry.

Conversely, he also delivered intended good to his minions. He joined disparate parts of the European wilds into one smoothly functioning empire that was protected by his widely flung garrisons. He had established a semblance of safety and certainty to these regions. Eumann smirked as he recalled all the shed blood that was necessitated for this to happen.

Finally, Eumann was tiring of even remotely chastising himself in thought or action. He finished with a hasty recall. He skimmed over the events of his later years as Septimius. He and his sons had foolishly gone to the hinterlands of civilization and attempted to take command of these unruly Picts. They resisted his dominant hand somehow, his spirit was bade go to Am Monadh, Septimius died in the Northern Isles there and his son's marched from these lands in indignation that the primitives of the vicinity in question had dared to overcome their Legions.

Now Eumann guffawed. Here he was making love to a royal Pictish woman . . . and loving every moment of it.

CHAPTER 14

Pairs In Love

Several nights had slipped by since Eumann had ruminated on his malevolent accomplishments as Mezopx and Septimius. This was not his bent at all now. He had performed all duties for Cinaed and had that behind him for the next twenty four hours. He and Catrione had not shared heat for a while and he was primed for her presence. And she had promised him that she would find some method to detach herself from Alpin. He was so desirous of her that he even mused on tearing this impediment limb from limb. Giving his identity away was disappearing into the recesses of his mind as worthy of having Catrione to himself exclusively.

Such human emotional needs meant that he was experiencing more layers of existence and he was ambivalent. The picking at the icy coatings around his heart was attractive to the degree that it lent him a higher level of tasting life It allowed him greater choices and he did tire of blood dripping, blood coalescing, blood iridescent, and blood infinitely. Though passion did not feed his cellular needs, it most certainly fed his spiritual needs. And that he had spiritual needs created a security, an underpinning for him that meant that there was a point to his formation beyond his own selfish cravings. He might be able to warm to that possibility over time.

For now though, he was very impatient for Catrione's presence. And he was aware that she was about to open and then climb down the hewn out steps and hasten to the oil lamp that was near at hand. He had blocked his vision of what she might be wearing as she came to him in their lair. This erected his hunger more so. Really though, her clothing on was of little interest to him as it rarely changed in style and color. But laying her bare of the quick layers always rendered him wanton and in love. She still caused some paralysis in him as she disrobed.

The lamp preceded her but it was she who lit up their tiny enclave. There was a shimmering, a luminescence that sang from her body and skin. It was here at this moment and had been thus every moment that they had entwined. He found that his heart and cock goaded him into all manner of actions with her. And she was privy to her effect upon him. She had that same power over most men; but this man she loved dearly.

He came to her and gently took the lamp from her hand and set it upon the ledge beside them. He let his fingers linger over her eyelids and then followed a descent down to her full formed lips. She was as treasure for him. Undead did not, after all, mean impervious. He trailed his fingers lower to that lovely curve of hers that traveled from delicate chin to the palpitations that he detected at the fragile concavity separating collar bone from collar bone. He traced his finger to an area of warmth beneath the garments.

As he did so, Catrione delicately began to divest herself of the cloak. Once the brooch was off, it slid casually off of her shoulders and arms with a single shrug of hers. His tracery continued at the initial upturn of her very abundant breasts there as she also began to lift her tunic from waist up. He stopped her hands though with a gesture that implied that he was to remove that garment himself. She dropped her arms immediately to her side and stood motionless. She was willing to be his slave in this session of theirs.

Simultaneous with the throbs of Eumann and Catrione's sublime foreplay, Aiobheean and Cinaed were tethering themselves to one another in their own cocoon of pleasure. Cinaed had waited until Catrione had left before he had departed himself. Alpin, once asleep, was a block that was beyond awakening this evening as Catrione had plied him with a lot of zythos. And he had been compliant in imbibing as much of the golden liquid as he could. Cinaed had acted as if asleep as soon as Eumann had completed their lessons. Therefore, his mother had not offered him a sip.

"Touch me, oh please touch me now," Aiobheean pleaded.

Eumann saw and heard their enfolding even during his near total fusion with Catrione.

She and Cinaed were at the lakeside of the Loch and infinitely more skilled this rendezvous than their first accidental encounter. He was amazed at how her mild panting breaths stirred his loins. She caressed his cheeks with the back of her fingers, then swept them outward and reached around his neck. Her hug made him dizzy with a fire that shot sharply into his rising cock. She leaned into that stir with her pelvis and undulated against him. He softly took her earlobe between his teeth and then whispered into her ear, "I love you."

She murmured back to him, "And I love you as well."

She dropped one hand to stroke the cockhead of his that protruded from his trews. He had parted from his tunic long ago. Her stroke rubbed his clear dew that was oozing from his cock all around and over his plum purple and massively swollen cockhead. His column seemed to elongate then into an even larger width and length.

She had taken him once. She was certain of her ability to do that again. Her maidenhead was split now and the pain would be milder. Yet she loved the pain that he unknowingly inflicted upon her as it built into a whorl of exquisitely explosive ecstasy.

Aiobheean pushed his trews down and they glided to his ankles where he kicked them away with one foot.

Eumann did not choose to ruin her tunic entirely; she had to wear it back to the wheelhouse. What he did though was to rip it about three quarters to Catrione's waist. It was relatively easy to do that too as the material had been stretched to a maximum by the thrust and weight of Catrione's chest. And with his maneuver, her breasts sprang to him and bobbled in his hands for an instant. He gazed at her huge mounds and they were beautiful to behold. He replaced his finger where he had removed it earlier. He drew his finger over the smooth rise to her aureole first and then her nipple. He had trailed this digit of his over the hint of a vein that flowed translucently to that deep brown and much contracted large aureole surrounding her firm thick caramel nipple. When he minutely touched that nipple it caused her to moan.

"My love, suck them, suck them hard. Do it immediately," she begged him. He obliged and drew her tip into his mouth. His tongue lashed at it. Her knees yielded just a fraction. He took her in his arms then and put her gracefully upon the flaxen covered straw bed.

Cinaed in parallel movement laid Aiobheean upon the sandy strip at their feet. She had already removed her tunic and her large breasts enticed Cinaed no end. Her globes were very full formed and upon their pale flesh stood gorgeous raspberry aureoles and hard berry colored pebbled nipples. He had tongued her there and twisted her nipples and was eager to do so again as it made Aiobheean writhe underneath him.

Aiobheean spread her legs wide and took her hands to open her nether lips to him. In his adolescent excitement, Cinaed had no patience for delicacy here and he simply plunged his massive tube into her. She lifted her hips to his thrust and he sank deep into her. An "ahhhhhh," escaped her lips and she wrapped her hands at the back of his neck. He moved in her harder and faster with each thrust. She experienced the vibration in her clit and the thrill throughout her vault with each pounding by him.

Eumann raised Catrione's hips so that she came to her all fours and he smoothly entered her from behind. Her opening was flooded and she moaned and threw her head back when he had lodged himself into her full length. His strokes accelerated and as he approached his threshold, he tangled his fingers in her hair and lightly pulled her head closer to him. Catrione trembled throughout as he did this. Her long curled locks made this tableau lush. Her breasts hung and shook with each contact of his pelvis with hers.

Cinaed flexed and sucked on her nipples as he drove into her. She now had her fingers on his clenching buttocks. He resisted his passion no longer and juiced her inner flesh with thick pearlescent jets of hot come. Aiobheean cried in her desire for his release and she released herself. Waves of delirious sensation came to her and her head rocked upward in automatic reflex. Both gasped in their vivid responses to one another. Cinaed brought himself to the sand next to her and placed his head upon her breast.

Simultaneously, the other pair in love found their own bliss. Catrione's orgasm sucked Eumann's juices out of him. He slid out of her; she touched herself there and then tasted her fingers sweetly.

CHAPTER 15

First Born

Aiobheean neared her time for birth. She felt resilient but tired easily. She bathed and rested some; she ran her hands over her much changed body. Her breasts were now much enlarged, were heavy almost beyond bearing and the blue veins were prominent. Her aureoles widened and deepened to a garnet color. Her nipples had become thickened and in constant state of erection and elongation. Aiobheean's belly had stretched taut and she was abundantly pregnant with child.

This child, who had to be a boy because of the manner he fought within her, jabbed her inside of her ribs many a time over the course of a day. Aiobheean watched as the babe inside rolled from right to left of her bulge there. She patted her stomach and sensed the instinctive stirrings in the heart of her motherhood.

Aiobheean's doula, Badb, had assisted many babies to come into the world and observed for signs that would announce the moments for Aiobheean to bring her child new life. She had helped deliver Aiobheean and she was to be critical in preparing Aiobheean's body before the travail was to begin.

Badb gave Aiobheean cream, skimmed from the top of goat's milk, and instructed her to rub, twist and work it well into her own nipples to toughen them and prepare them for plenty of infant suckling. In addition, Badb demonstrated to Aiobheean how to rub a portion of the same cream into her entrance between her legs. She told Aiobheean to use her fingers to gently stretch that area in order to create suppleness and permit easier birthing.

Touching herself comforted Aiobheean as she no longer had Cinaed to ask to ply his fingers there. She applied the lotion and smiled; albeit sadly as she recalled the times that Cinaed had sought those same regions in their passion.

Badb gave Aiobheean the freedom to be herself and to pad through her daily routine. Yet she was never far away on the premise that labors onset was to arrive shortly. The birthing area in the wheelhouse had been designated to give Aiobheean the privacy that she required to focus on the work at hand.

This morning, the yellow orb, bright in the cerulean sky shined on. Aiobheean was bright herself. She hummed in indistinct melody as she gathered furs, flaxen material and feathers for their warmth and softness. She appeared to be collecting material as if to build a nest. Badb took notice of this and saw that Aiobheean's belly appeared lower and her breasts seemed fuller under her tunic, making the material stretched and taut.

A little later in that day, when the sun had just snuck past its zenith, Badb viewed Aiobheean returning from a stroll. Her hands reposed upon her belly and she had a quizzical hint to her face. The aide went to Aiobheean and asked, "Are you feeling something my mother to be?"

"This belly has taken on a life of its own, my doula! Just seconds ago as I was walking, my bulge grew tight and pushed out to here." Aiobheean indicated even further elongation of the stomach that had become huge.

"Are you feeling pain?"

"No pain there, just tightness." Aiobheean replied.

"The occasion for this child's birth may be closer than we imagine. Bathe and get some rest. Definitely, do not stray far from the wheelhouse my young mother. Always let me know where you will be traipsing off to, please!" the doula mildly implored.

Badb went off to find the items that were to support Aiobheean to relax and grind through the pain that was like no other that she might ever experience. Unlike Cinaed, Badb planned on being at Aiobheean's side to offer reinforcement and catch this first born as the bundle fell into waiting hands.

Three uneventful cycles of the sun passed by as Aiobheean continued to assemble and arrange the wool, fur and the flax material into a nest worthy of multiple births. She spent her days going about her customary activities with Badb mostly in sight. Periodically, she paused to feel that tightness in her womb occur once again. She lifted her tunic to check the movement and saw her protruding abdomen rise, firm up and appear as if it were forming a point and then quiet and soften again. She was intrigued by this occurrence. These painless contractions were increasing in their frequency and she was certain that her time was imminent.

After fitful slumber, she awoke the next morning with remembrance of positive dreams in her sleep overnight. She had dreamt of Cinaed being near her and wrapping his arms about her and the infant that they held together. The dream was wonderful, the reality less so. Cinaed was gone. And she was helpless to change that. She longed for him and for their lives to have been different. She sighed so deeply then.

Aiobheean began the fresh routine of spreading the cream upon her expanded nipples. During this ritual, as she rubbed in the lotion and twisted and turned her deeply reddened elongated fingers of flesh, her abdomen constricted and a contraction began. This wave was unlike the others in that there was pain in the midst of the constriction. Aiobheean's eyes flashed wide open and she shifted her hands to her navel. This pain lasted longer than the rest and she knew.

When she went to place the cream to her opening, at the edge of the opening, there was a roundness crowning. It was yellowish white and streaked with brilliant red blood. The blend here produced a stickiness that Badb had prepared her for. Her heart quickened when she realized that her time for bearing this child was, indeed, very close. Aiobheean hurriedly finished her ablutions and firmly decided not to venture from the wheelhouse today at all. She sought Badb out and the doula exclaimed, "Yes, most certainly the time is about upon us."

This particular day was one of watchfulness and anticipation; the waiting felt endless. Aiobheean attempted to settle in her bed but her heart was filled with an anxiety at what was soon to be. The waves were now unceasing, though not in a regular pattern. Aiobheean remained smiling and talking and in motion nonetheless. Badb kept Aiobheean company and when the contractions came, felt her belly.

"The waiting and the intense strain that your body is undertaking until the infant arrives is the hardest part."

Aiobheean and Badb were playing a little game that they had devised with small stones and sticks for purposes of distraction. Aiobheean felt thirsty of a sudden and stood to get a cup of water. It was then that she sensed the liquid from inside her trickle down her legs. She peered down at the ground and then back up to Badb, repeated this action again, and searched the doula's face intently.

"I did not feel the need to pass my water, doula. What is happening?"

Badb clapped her hands and a crooked smile crossed her face. She reassured Aiobheean that this was expected. "The babe will begin its journey very soon my lovely young mother! Passing the water is always a sign."

No sooner had Badb given her explanation when mildly serosanguinous fluid rushed from between her legs and splashed to the floor's surface where a puddle instantly was produced.

Badb clapped her wrinkled hands again. "It is that time! Oh yes, it is time! Come Aiobheean! We shall prepare you and soon you will meet your child!"

Parturition progressed steadily and Aiobheean was much more comfortable in her activity now. She paced and then steadied herself on a large stone when the squeezing pain gripped her abdomen. The doula encouraged her to breathe and put pressure on Aiobheean's back. That eased some of the internal force occurring and reduced the pain that Aiobheean was presently experiencing.

Badb observed that Aiobheean was still smiling and chattering between the pains, so she continued her encouragement that the laboring woman in front of her walk as she felt able.

Aiobheean's pains came closer together and the smiles had totally disappeared. She was panting and resting often to grimace and withstand the pain. Badb remained very close to the obviously distressed woman.

"Make way to the birthing room. Nature speaks to us now and her voice is loud."

Aiobheean's parents held to the background as was the tradition of the Gaelic culture. All was left to the expertise of the doula in this eventful period. And, here and now, her parents were glad of their culture's rigid rules in this regard.

Other than Aiobheean's gatherings, the birthing room was sparse except for a U shaped stone seat that was fairly low to the floor. There were indentations carved out of the sides where Aiobheean's hands would grasp to give her leverage and a security of touch as well. Badb, steadfast aid that she was, was proximate to Aiobheean.

Aiobheean was strong but given to crying out during her contractions. On the other side of the walls, one was able to hear her guttural moans and calling out for Cinaed.

Badb whispered to her, "Aio, save your strength. You will need it as your child's birth approaches more so." The doula massaged Aiobheean's belly gently and offered her soothing tea in tiny sips. The aroma of the leaves, which were lemony, quelled Aiobheean's cries temporarily.

Her moans became louder and Aiobheean was up and down, pacing to and fro. The anguish that her eyes reflected told Badb that it was the moment! "Sit here, Aiobheean! Listen to me now! Put your hands in these curved in places and when the next strike of pain comes, bear down with all of your might." Aiobheean nodded with a mixed look of fear and determination.

In the seat now, Badb assisted her with the removal of her tunic, so that it did not interfere. Another piercing pain lanced Aiobheean again.

"Ohhhhhh! Aggghhhh! It's happening now! Unnnghhh!"

"Push down, Aio! Push now!"

Aiobheean bore down with all of her remaining strength. Her face was ashen and without any rosy glow. Hers was a reddened hot face, full of grit and will!

"Again!" cried Badb, "Push again, dear mother!" The doula mopped her forehead with a damp cloth and returned to her place on the floor.

Pushing and bearing down, Aiobheean continued to struggle to bring her baby from her womb.

"I see its head emerging. Again, young mother, one more big push!"

"Badbbbbbbb!" she screamed! And then with one large effort, the baby slipped out of her. "Ohhhhhhhh! Ohhhhhh!" she was spent and fell back into the seat, resting against the wall and closing her eyes.

It was then that she heard the first cry; a hearty wail from the babe. She kept her eyelids compressed together for an instant as tears welled up and then dripped a salty trail descending to her chin. What joy there was in the hearing of the cries of emergence into this world!

"Open your eyes young mother and rest them . . . . upon your son!"

Badb lifted this bundle, all sticky and wet and set him on his mother's breasts. She gazed at him lovingly, cradling him in her arms; Constantine, she had decided on Constantine earlier but was sure in this moment as she observed him. He repositioned his ruddy face and instinctively found a nipple where he began to suckle softly. Aiobheean beamed his direction, closed her eyes once again and filled herself full of Cinaed. What would it be to him to be aware that he had a son; a tiny yet but very strong son? This one was destined for great events Aiobheean was certain.

Badb once again had successfully pressed her skills upon Aiobheean in order to bring forth another into life.

The cord that tied mother to child was unnecessary and the doula tied it with flaxen string she had pulled from Aiobheean's tunic and then had soaked in an astringent made with woad flowers. The cord was cut with a small blade that she constantly carried with her for exactly this purpose. She cleaned both mother and child with an herbal preparation of chamomile and woad. Then she covered them with furs.

It was only then, when all was secured, that she paced from the room in order to leave mother and son to bond.

She announced to Aiobheean's parents that they had a healthy and beautiful grandson.

CHAPTER 16

Her Reformation

She was awash in tears that dampened her cheeks profusely. He wiped at them with fingers drawn and cradled her head in the crook of his arm. He had just lovingly explained to her the wonderful potential of her possible reformation into eternal flesh and dominance aplenty.

She had fixated upon his words as he honored her with the offer of a gift beyond reckoning.

And he had just exposed himself to her as a vampire.

Her liquid clear diamonds spilled from her eyes and Eumann was not capable of reading her here. Were these a sign of gladness, fear, sorrow or a mix of any or all?

Catrione was beginning to sob yet linked her hand in his. She curled her fingers at his knuckles and stroked his palms thumb wise. Her intermittent choking gasps for air reached to and into his heart. He clasped her to him and compressed her to his chest, then nuzzled her cheek with his in spite of her moistness dampening his skin quickly.

Eventually she settled as he rocked her gently. She was soothed and spoke to him, nearly in control of her words. His instinct as he rested his chin lightly over her curls was that she was bursting with joy at his offering. She paused just longer and whispered, "Suckle at my neck. Let me react to the hot touch of your teeth upon me!"

She bent her head left as he swung his to the right. She presented to him a special location on her body that he imagined was exquisitely sensitive for her. He brushed her there with the smooth enamel of his fangs. He was deliciously gentle as those fangs were as sharp as a razor's edge and he did not wish to pierce her supple skin whatsoever. And not the slightest trickle of the crimson appeared under his oral tracery. She extended her proffered neck to him as fully as possible now and Eumann trailed his hot tongue delicately along that proffered sloping neck.

"Take me, please, take me and turn me!"

"I must have you before I have you my sweet and wonderful Catrione.

I need for you to be cognizant that I may only turn those that I care about. And further, I hold you in a regard beyond my prior imagining. It is that I so much more than care about you. I cherish you and find your presence before me and in my life inestimable.

Turn and kiss me please!"

Catrione did exactly that and their lips joined barely but the spark furnished a supreme arousal that streaked immediately to both of their loins. He took her buttocks in his cupped hands, dug his digits into pliant flesh and forced her hips and groin into his bulge. Then he eased his fingers from her flesh that were momentarily imprinted and swept his palms only over the smooth glide that her rear provided.

She was wholly nude and he had his trews on still. His cock climb was massive and throbbing in a burn of hoped for satisfaction that was rapidly overtaking him. He stepped away from her then and, as if casually, ripped the under wear in half. His shaft defied gravity as if such a power did not exist. Their gaze was cast upon the other with a rapt intensity that sliced through the dimmest of light. The oil lamp flickered but with ever diminishing flare.

He grasped his manhood and squeezed it hard and next stroked it as if in slow motion. He spread wider and bent slightly at the knees as she came to him.

She was magnetized and kneeled before his prod, took his bulbous cockhead in her mouth and positioned her hand upon his. They both gripped his shaft tightly and used a steady hard rhythm up and down his length.

His thighs were shaking as a quivering bowstring might have once loosened from the arrow. This minute shivering of his, he realized, stirred her magnificently. She lusted for his weakness-revealed that was created by his passion for her. She moaned as she licked and sucked him, feeling and skimming his tremble with outthrust fingers of her remaining hand.

She followed his thighs curvature upward and clasped his tight sack and shocked him utterly as she then lightly rubbed the area between his balls and anal opening. The sharp and lovely jolt of her touch there pushed an exhalation from him.

He leaned against the wall and arched his shaft into her mouth more fully where her tongue lashed at his swollen organ.

He was wild at her continued play upon his cock. He had to feel her surround his tool without any more hesitation. He had to have her now! So he seized her cheeks, stopped her motion altogether and extended her head slightly so that she had to peer into his flaming eyes.

"Sit upon me!"

He rushed to the bed and sat with his legs outstretched, spread and his thick instrument beckoning her. She squatted down to his manhood and guided him into her slick wetness as she faced away from him. She planted hands on his knees and reared back into him repeatedly. She moaned with her motion on him and drove herself sharper, faster and with pounding vibration as she recoiled off his pelvis.

She was faint with desire for his come, her come, the march of booming ecstasy that was fierce upon them.

She panted and suddenly sensed as his large hands cupped her vast dangling mounds and hard nipples. This became her tripwire and then his. She spasmed on his shaft and threw her head back simultaneously. Her moans escalated to cries. Her orgasm was beyond any intensity she had ever experienced before. She was conscious of nothing but the ever engulfing avalanche of sensation within her.

His seed burst from deep inside his testicles and shot and gushed from his jerking cock that fit within her perfectly.

He took her neck then in a paroxysm of stunning desire. He ravaged her carotid and tasted the finest of blood. It was magic and he gulped as he jetted his come into her. He gulped as she was consumed by waves of her own.

It was thus that Catrione too was transformed into the infinite twilight of the undead.

The timing of this was perfect beyond belief for Catrione. Alpin had taken a younger woman to his bed. Catrione had been cast aside. He would no longer pay any attention to her constant nighttime absences. Her loss was so her gain this occasion. Internally, she rejoiced.

Cinaed noticed but underwent such agitation regarding her that he was vastly relieved at her permanent departure.

CHAPTER 17

Backward Looking

He was a bit older and a slightly seasoned soldier; he had already participated in and survived several clashes with numerous neighbors, especially the Picts. He had aged six years since his entry into manhood. He remembered the wildcat well though.

The year was eight hundred thirty one A.D. and he marveled at his rich future with his Dal Riatan comrades. A single blemish shaded the shining skin of an otherwise most auspicious body of personal fortune.

That blemish was similar to a sliver that one had located but for the life of him was powerless in forcing it out and away. That sliver, though seemingly innocuous and inconspicuous, left a pain whose ache captured all attention. The almost unseen became the ruler of Cinaed's mind. He ran from it perpetually and, lo, it clung to him and was his ceaseless companion.

It was thus that he sought to divest himself of the memory of Aiobheean. He shook the specter repeatedly, waving the finger of his pain vigorously. How does one manage to shake a thoroughly embedded sliver from its impaled location? One does not, one cannot shake it away. And Cinaed was no exception.

King Alpin, father and current leader of their clan and larger territory of Dal Riata, was oblivious to the inner turmoil that his son had and was experiencing. Alpin and Cinaed loomed large on the precipice edge as the two surveyed Alpin's kingdom. And Alpin exclaimed forcefully and with grand sweep of one arm what was Alpin's and what should become Cinaed's as Alpin's eventual successor kin. Cinaed's long and unruly hair rustled from and around his face as his father spoke and as Cinaed scanned the horizon that was theirs.

Eumann was party to all in the past and present as his invading vision had escalated with the nurture and practice that he had vigorously continued. The impending future remained in disparate blurred fragments but that too was slowly progressing. Eumann, therefore, vividly discerned the emotional tension and grief that was omnipresent for Cinaed. Aiobheean was at the harsh center of it.

He and Cinaed had even had a brief exchange about the younger's heartache; it was very short lived as Cinaed insisted on blocking the subject after only several statements. If he had gone on, Eumann would have had to have comforted Cinaed as Cinaed was on the verge of sobbing as it was. The only manly approach was to cease and desist talking upon the subject! That they both did!

What Eumann perceived was this; that Cinaed loved Aiobheean with every fiber of his being. It had been one of those things that had befallen Cinaed in his first glance at Aiobheean as she meandered through the city streets those several years past. He had been smitten and mightily so. That was to be Cinaed's only genuine love while he lived.

Yet, concomitantly, Cinaed was such an impulsive being as well. His instant reactions determined so much of his behavior. He was well served by his rapid decision making in battle but this mode of his was met less kindly in his personal domain. Thus Eumann watched him closely in order to provide that protective shield that Cinaed occasionally required. It was Eumann's duty; Eumann's master wove that understanding through Eumann, to see that Cinaed came to his bright and later days in fullness and health. He had saved him once as a boy about to become man; he must do the same for the adult if sharp need ever arose again.

One season past, Aiobheean had taken Cinaed's hand and stroked it over her fulsome abdomen. She then ceased her guided stroke of his hand when she knew that his hand laid over her umbilicus. He froze. They were not compelled to wait long for the kicking of their joined creation within her developed womb.

Whether it was the jolt to his hand from the active fetus that ignited Cinaed's response or a fear of fatherhood itself, Eumann, in spite of his rigorous abilities as a vampire seer, was not capable of ferreting out the nuances within Cinaed regarding that instant negative flare of his. And was it even necessary to be cognizant of the reasons anyhow. Sometimes the field of mystery just had to stay fallow.

Cinaed's response told all. Nothing beyond that had to be discerned.

Cinaed had almost stumbled in his hurry to get away from her belly.

The backward looking bent of Cinaed's mind now, always his obsession but never his wish, revealed over and over the surprise that both he and Aiobheean underwent with his silent startle to the budding baby within her.

Aiobheean had flinched perceptibly at Cinaed's wide eyed rearward lurch and hot removal of his palm from the area of her body most beloved by her. She gasped and fearfully queried him, "Have you no desire to be a father? You must have seen the rising up and swelling there before this?"

Cinaed stuttered out, "I have experienced only nineteen annual cycles. What do I know?! I am not ready for this! I have not even marched to war once with my father yet!

I crave you and love you so my Aiobheean but you must do this alone. I am departing you and this immediately!"

Cinaed could not, would not, prevent these words from being uttered by him. He was in shock as was Aiobheean. But he was no more in control of his actions than was the moon in its circuit.

He fled his life love in her hour of need. He fled her and left her stunned, in grave consternation and she stood weeping at his abandonment of her and the babe!

This was not her Cinaed!

This was not happening!

She too raced, as a six month pregnant woman could, from the Loch shore to the wheelhouse and straight into the arms of her equally astounded parent's embrace!

Aiobheean's family was not only high born but of elevated sophistication over much of the Dal Riatan populace. They worshipped the singular Christian God that Columba had bestowed upon the heathen in prior times. The three proceeded to their tiny indoor nave that housed enough space for a rudimentary crucifix and a floor to kneel upon. They kneeled and all murmured their prayers for a return to sanity of Cinaed.

Aiobheean nearly collapsed between her father and mother and was inconsolable.

As a matter of fact, Eumann recognized, so was Cinaed.

CHAPTER 18

Easter Sunday

Many in Dal Riata were hunkered down or asleep in their shelters, on this Easter Sunday of eight hundred thirty four Anno Domini, praying that Alpin was to be victorious in what was to evolve into a large confrontation with his Pictish neighbors. This was Alpin's battle and he was planning on taking it to them in an abundance of swift ferocity. He was front and center of his warriors and his boldness and determination resonated even in the deeper moments of night as they slid through one of the valleys of the Grampian Mountains.

His spies had informed him of Viking incursions into Pictish territory and the beginning decimation of the Pictish population. Alpin was gleeful at this news and took it as an opportunity to wreak further havoc upon his wife's kinsmen.

Alpin was Gaelic to his soul and was brutal to all Picts who crossed his path. Catrione was spared singly for her splendid outward appearance. Alpin had lusted for her instantly. All else regarding the strong and capable Catrione's humanity was dismissed; actually not even dismissed. To dismiss something, one had to consider the item first and then roust it out of the mind's attention. There was nothing then to dismiss as Alpin never posited the thought in the first place.

Eumann had done what he rarely chose and that was to take up his sword and stand shoulder to shoulder with Alpin and Cinaed this episode.

Eumann was a skilled and dexterous warrior in his own right. With his acquired vampire powers, he was nearly invincible. For the reason of his abilities, not aware of his vampire addition, Alpin had been thoroughly provoked by Eumann's prior absences in battle. So, somewhat by necessity, Eumann stormed out with the rest of the vast Gaelic forces to contribute his best. It was unwise to draw Alpin's attention upon him for several reasons; most especially that he might have to reveal his identity were Alpin to study him too closely. And for the sake of simplicity, he wanted his connection with Catrione to remain in the dark also. He found he now dodged messiness if he had a choice.

The most important motive however for accompanying Alpin was to see to Cinaed's safety and survival. This was Cinaed's initial incursion into significant Dal Riatan combat. He had been involved in small raids. This was no raid though. Alpin intended to obliterate the Picts once and for all.

It was the dead of night and fortunate that the Gaelic men in arms knew their land. Torches assisted to a degree but were not relied upon as minimal light was required to engage the enemy in a surprise embrace.

Alpin was not cognizant of what Eumann was. Eumann may have been uninformed as to the outcome of these events arriving shortly except that the Picts had been apprised of the Gael's forward march and were to be met with equal fierceness as Alpin planned for the Picts. Spies lurked everywhere: Pictish were as common and competent as Gaelic. Catrione was most certainly not of that ilk.

Not only were the Picts prepared, they had an array of their own ready to swarm upon the Gaels. There had been some unintentional misinformation and the Picts had not been as hamstrung by the Vikings as had been told to Alpin. They were established within several vales overlooking the valley up which the Gaels were proceeding. The Pictish were hungry for slaughter on a par with Alpin.

Eumann was not perturbed whatsoever. His power was to be the deciding factor in the outcome here. He was so confident of that. He had darkness as his ally so that he had full opportunity to unleash his full might and not be discovered. This was to be the true surprise for the Picts.

His love for Catrione swayed him not either. She was lush, welcoming and refined. Her people were often not. He had his fangs at the ready and relished the idea of the Pictish assault and then their fear and trembling as thousands of their necks would be scored with his mark. He was beyond confident; he was absolute in his certainty.

War whoops, shrieks and brandishing of weapons blew down upon them and now all Gaels sprang to their own defense. Blades were embedded into vulnerable flesh, swords clanged against shields and fists rained against one another in the melee.

Eumann had his long sword drawn as did Alpin and Cinaed. Bodies already piled at father and son's feet. Cinaed swung and jabbed with his bloodied sword in comparable skill, strength and focus as his vastly more experienced father.

Alpin goaded his son on with cries of exhortation and Cinaed returned the same back to Alpin. They were connected on the string of battle euphoria. Their swords whirred through midnight air and then sank into barbarian's tattooed flesh. Moans of the wounded and dying surrounded them and were ever mounting amongst the enemy. Yet Gaels collapsed frequently before the Pictish onslaught also. And the Pictish hoard kept coming as their number seemed limitless.

Eumann had to act swiftly even if it meant losing actual sight of Cinaed for minutes. And minutes was all that it would take. Besides, Cinaed seemed very adequate at the task of mayhem, murder and destruction. He and Alpin were frightening in their individual warrior's success. But how long were the other still fighting Gaels to last? He planned to not leave that question in the offing any longer!

The wild blond hair-spiked, woad painted brute fighting before him fell torso first and then his now stilled head flew to a distance as a blur crushed his carotid and spat out the remains to the ground.

Separation of head from body via an explosion of gore and spurting crimson from neck after neck became a repetitious onslaught against the Pictish combatants. Gaels were beyond stunned as the greater number of Pictish soldiers shrank rapidly. The surviving Picts were beyond stunned to the point that many froze in mid sword stroke, comprehending their worst nightmare in that instant. And in that instant, many Gaels thrust death strokes into their immobile antagonists.

Blood of the enemy flowed freely.

Pictish retreat began in a panic. Some even inadvertently breathed their last as they tumbled into the blades of their own comrades behind them. Soon there was chaotic motion as the lucky pounded up the vales where they had come from and desperately surmounted the mountain passes to escape the ravages of this battle.

Eumann, Cinaed and Alpin raised their swords as they recognized victory. Waves of upward thrust swords and hollers of pride and joy ensued from the rest.

The vampire perceived now that Oengus II had perished in this terrible skirmish.

CHAPTER 19

Pride Before the Fall

At the juncture of the vales and valley, two routes climbed to passes that permitted individuals to reenter their Pictish homeland. As if in a herd, the conglomeration of terrified tattooed soldiers fled behind one another on a single narrow dirt ribbon that ran more sharply upward but was in close proximity to the scene of the massacre. Had Oengus II survived there, the rout and following retreat would have led up both paths so that Alpin would have had to part his warriors in two at least; or so the Gaels assumed. As it was, the entire Gaelic hoard only had to charge up behind those in withdrawal and slice them to death, jump over those gored corpses and perform the same repeatedly.

Yet the Picts and the dead Oengus II had a further surprise.

Eumann encouraged Alpin to let the Picts wail and flee. Their shattered numbers attested to the absolute success of the Gaels mission. Though the enemy was not obliterated, they were helpless and cowed now. Let the few still upon their feet go. They were not about to remain a challenge to the mighty Alpin and his forces.

Alpin was not even remotely interested in Eumann's courtesies. The King perceived that this was the ripe moment for eliminating the reoccurring threat that the Picts had posed to the Dal Riatans over the years. No more of that, Alpin raged. They were never going to haunt the Gaelic territories again. And Alpin was going to demonstrate his strategic genius as well.

Cinaed agreed with his father and turned a harsh stare at Eumann for the weak and cowardly suggestion. Cinaed was willing to fight on at the mere gesture of his father's hand to move through the rocky terrain after the treacherous heathen. His mother may have been of this breed but he had grave doubts about her loyalty, at least to his father, and was not ever to yield to her kin. His mother was beautiful but that persuaded him not at all. Actually, her beauty confounded him and created a lust which he repressed and found disturbing. His sword, not his cock, was his instrument on the battle field.

Alpin pointed to Cinaed and Cinaed immediately lead his phalanx to the track that rose more moderately. His duty was to reach the ridge and down before the enemy so that his men would be able to hack the Picts apart as they shot from their path's exit. Alpin leapt up the other trail with his phalanx shadowing him tightly. His group would kill many and Cinaed's would decimate the rest.

Eumann was fatigued by all of the carnage that had confronted him. He had chosen to savagely tear victory from the Pictish majority. He loved his brute strength. But he was hopelessly finding himself tied to the notion that there existed a balance in this world. Extremes of behavior were grounded in a misguided sense that simplicity of idea dictated outcomes. It was not a simple existence and he was yielding to that fact the longer that he absorbed bits of wisdom. His years had been many and those bits had accumulated. He was to have no more of any butchery tonight.

At that he swung around and strode away from the receding Gaelic savages. He left them to their deeds. He was ashamed of them without a doubt.

The darkness had come to her and Eumann earlier. Catrione rose from her demon sleep and stretched. Eumann left abruptly and joined with Alpin and Cinaed. She contracted of a sudden upon recognition of his immediate absence. She was routinely hidden now; and presently hidden from the fighting as she roused. She heard the noise though and it was the sounds of blood being spilt and corpses that toppled onto one another. More than the screams of the warriors, she listened to the cries of those being hunted. She was most especially in anguish over the sound of her truest love, Eumann

Catrione assumed imminent doom for Eumann and she sent a thought to him. This thought more than suggested, craved, that he steal away so they could be together. Even mere minutes would give them an eternity of remembered sentiment were something dire to occur to him! She pleaded with Eumann in this psychic way and knew that he heard it as a voice sounding clearly; she begged him.

Her entreaty was unnecessary as Eumann had already faced away from his comrades in arms.

He smiled as he heard it echo within the interior walls of his cranium. It was delicious and the right thing to do. And he let her words repeat themselves over and over as he flew to her. "Ohh, Eumann, my one and only love. Make it possible to come to me and be with me for a fraction. I will lock you into my heart one more time and let it be there forever. Please my love, grant me this. I sense the harm that surrounds you. I cannot bear another second without you. I am wanton to touch you and touch your heart. The horror and cruelty of this war is beyond my ability to endure . . .

unless you appease me here and now. Heed my call and desire. You will never regret it. I love you so."

He sought her as he had to taste her sweetness in this otherwise foul foray of Alpin's.

"Catrione," Eumann spoke from his mind's power source, "Meet me at the edge of the tunnel, make your way outside of it and crouch down, so as to be as invisible as possible. I am approaching you even now. When I swoop down toward you, transform and wing with me to a darkened spot in the meadow that I will choose. I hurry as no one must find the tunnel or see you in that location. Be ready for me!"

Catrione heard and understood and went to the edge of the tunnel. She lifted the sod and crept low to the ground.

Outside, it was pitch black, save for the stars that shone above the mist. She heard him arriving, morphed to bat form and became horizon bound with Eumann.

The meadow approached and they rode down upon it. Instant transformation flashed through them both and he took her face into his hands and began kissing her from eyelash to trembling chin. The tears fell from her eyes and wet her cheeks ever so. He tasted her salt diamonds as he kissed her there and then kissed her everywhere.

She was livid with desire and anticipation.

Their lips met and they explored with tongues searching. They wished for a burn so large that every second would be captured in their memories.

Eumann's cock was erect, beating and pulsing in his sheer desire for her. He tore at her tunic and she was hot and prepared for his entering of her. He grabbed forcefully at her breasts as he was afflicted with an unruly passion.

Eumann picked Catrione up and steadied himself against a large standing rock. He lifted her higher and she opened her legs wide and wrapped herself around his waist within the concave space at his lower back that was between him and the granite slab. He searched out her glistening center and glowing bud and slowly dropped her down upon himself; he then fixed her there, hard. He lifted her hips up and then lowered them as he stroked deep into her. Her arms were clasped over his neck and she whimpered and experienced consuming heat from his great need for her. He bent his torso slightly to her and moved her hips harder and faster.

He sensed the explosion of passion primed to erupt. Catrione bit her lip so as to restrain her cries. They melded and Eumann's steady spurting of lava-like semen filled her. It scorched so that she came to her climax fiercely. And then she came some more. They panted in unison and were as if fused within their embrace.

Suddenly, Eumann's vision swept through him. The hair at the back of his neck pricked at him acutely. He felt a sharp pain in his carotid as well. Alpin, he is finished! What of Cinaed?! He remains just alive!

"Transform yourself my love. Wing to the tunnel instantly and remain! Promise me!"

She saw Alpin and Cinead also. Direness had come to them instead of to Eumann.

Without sweet kisses of any kind, Eumann blurred from her arms and was gone.

Catrione took to the blackened sky herself and went as he had commanded.

CHAPTER 20

Higher Power

It had been an enormous trap with throngs of Pictish grunts holding; waiting for that precise instant to bury the Gaels in their own arrogance, pride and certainty. As it so happened for the Gaels, the tableau of bloodshed and unmitigated stupidity ultimately cost them many of their own lost lives. Only mysterious forces rang in their eventual feeble victory. Even that bit of luck salvaged only a portion of the accomplishment that Alpin had sought in the devising of this clash.

Eumann was observing the massacre as he remained sky bound; and this massacre of the Gaels had been pursued by Alpin and Cinaed with relish. They had had a reasonable plan though. How much more cleanly could a plan with a positive outcome for them have been devised? It had seemed brilliant; pinch the retreating stream of Picts between a rearward onslaught and a frontal assault simultaneously and squeeze them into oblivion. This rendered the annihilation of the enemy a foregone conclusion . . . . almost.

Eumann had been distracted by the solidity of Alpin's plan, the antipathy he felt for the final brutality upon the already seeming decimated Picts and, most especially making the first two pale and bland in comparison, his rash and hot want for midnight meadow lovemaking with Catrione.

Otherwise, he would have perceived the true occurrence and then the final outcome upon the battlefield.

He had not seen it upcoming and so was now silently circling the darkened horizon above waiting the command of his higher power to tell him how to staunch the flow of blood that Alpin and Cinaed were undergoing.

Seconds passed, critical seconds, and he sensed nothing from his single power which, other than the sun, silver and the piercing terminal ache of a wooden stake to his heart, he answered to. What must be affirmed by this higher power exclusively focused upon the survival or demise of Alpin and Cinaed here. Would it be that both were to be lost, both saved or only one of the two was to stand amongst the flesh strewn everywhere?

What happened to Eumann then was that his required message from his unseen entity arrived. An invisible weight pressed upon his back and the winged form that he was shot a straight line of descent aimed at Cinaed. Alpin could not be ignored but was ignored. Eumann, and only the primeval beast had the capacity for doing this, sheered through Cinaed's skin and meshed with his cells and synapses. Eumann's shell was deposited standing shoulder to shoulder with Cinaed. Eumann was vividly alive, just without the energy that he had experienced since eight hundred and eleven.

The Pictish warrior who was about to stab Cinaed and most assuredly would have slain him in the next second was himself stabbed frontally by Eumann. The Pict died in that moment disbelieving that he had not regarded Eumann's presence until it was beyond the dying man's control.

Cinaed was now inhabited as Eumann was not and it reinvigorated Cinaed. He perceived that his father was in the severe throes of a singlehanded standoff against a surrounding multitude of the woad colored enemy. Cinaed shifted his gaze to locate his father precisely. When his gaze found him, Cinaed's knees nearly buckled him to the ground's already bloody surface.

The ancient vampire, who was now involuntarily hosted within a new body, and Cinaed together were stunned at the sight. But the undead entity pulled Cinaed up from what appeared to others for an instant as if Cinaed were on the verge of collapse.

Other eyes followed Cinaed's eyes and what they collectively viewed brought a shattering anguish, yet paradoxically, renewed their determination and enthusiasm to beat back their foe. They had just glimpsed their King's head spiked through with a sword up to its hilt and that sword was now hoisted above the massed Pictish hoard that encircled the offending warrior with Alpin's head. The stump of his neck was ragged with oozing vessels and rent flesh. The rigor beginning kept Alpin's dead eyes wide open as if he was horrified at his own demise. It was a trick of death but had its huge impact nonetheless. Alpin's head bobbed up and down as it was spat upon, jeered and poked at.

Cinaed shrieked at the vision and thumped his slashed and crimson bare chest. Though war was evil, this was an effrontery even to the values of war, or so Cinaed felt. Cinaed went mad in this moment and did not even have to resort to the powers of the vampire within; though that gave him manifest strength that he was not aware of.

His blade stung, maimed, ravished and put to rest a swath of the enemy before him.

The enemy had outsmarted the Gaels even as the Gaels plundered them fore and aft in the early stages of this battle. To Alpin, the butchery was an awesome spectacle and he foolishly waded in with an excess that doomed him.

Cinaed's vampire had a flash consideration that he had once been as cruel as Alpin.

What Alpin had not anticipated nor did Cinaed or their comrades expect was an ambush-ready and hungrily waiting Pictish phalanx poised for hours at the mouth of the trailhead where the combat now raged. Cleverly, these Picts had used only a portion of their fighters in their initial attack. A mass had been reserved, primed for the Gaels to succumb to the bait. And succumb they did.

Oengus II smiled from above and truly had only wanted his men to flee up one trail. This had been a plan of his creation from the beginning.

While Gael backs were turned in their own venomous slaughter of those deemed the Pictish full force, the enemy's other numbers set upon the Gaels from behind. They shouted gleefully as they ran forward and hacked the unprepared Gaels into their demise and death.

That was the grisly scene that Eumann had lowered himself down to.

Now, as Cinaed drew blood and slew so many in his wrathful rage, his troops roused themselves and reengaged with a fury that matched Cinaed's and forced the Picts into their second retreat of this night. This retreat was genuine and the disorganized array had no idea of whether they were tailed at all. They did not analyze that whatsoever; they simply ran mindlessly to what they hoped was close at hand safety somewhere ahead. It was pell-mell and the Gaels were certain of their dominance this round.

They searched and discovered Alpin's head. Then they wrapped and secured it. One soldier protected it closely as it was cherished by all.

Their leader was no longer Alpin. Cinaed had numerous reasons for concluding this engagement. First, one act of impulsive and mistaken audacity was not going to happen again. Cinaed was altered and this was a second source of the cessation of their aggression. The death of his father had turned him from more immediate blood as well. Enough had presently been shed; their own and his enemies' definitely. They were far from home and the gravely lessened amount of survivors was the final issue that convinced one and all to return as best as they were able.

The wounds were numerous and the fatigue was vast. Yet they had, in the end, conquered.

The slog to Dal Riata was long and difficult in the physical condition that they possessed. But the embrace of that city was impetus for limping in through their city gates and to be greeted as victors. This was appropriate as they considered themselves victors.

Cinaed led them through to and into the city. This was the position that he was to take permanently. All knew and approved of that. All that remained was the feast upcoming and the coronation whose formality was to announce to the world who was the new Dal Riatan King.

Steeped in darkness, so much had transpired.

CHAPTER 21

Mead's Influence

Eumann, the undead Cinaed and the victorious Gaelic survivors, upon their ragged march through the gates of the city, were determined to harvest their conquest in the only manner known to them. They were to feast, drink, toast themselves and then let all of Dal Riata participate as they wished. The time to assuage their grief over Alpin's death and to care for their battle fatigue was to come later.

They were so determined to celebrate now; until they could do that no longer. The occasions for a lusty gathering of the entire populace were rare in the harsh era that etched itself into each raw day where subsistence was often scarcely eked out. This was an extraordinary moment. They had overcome their astonishment at the Pictish numbers and full preparedness for the Gaelic incursion. And though the images of the mysterious ruthlessness by which many of their foes had been slaughtered sat heavy, they let that concern vanish as if they had never been privy to the witnessing of such an event.

Now they were ready to play, dance and carouse until they dropped to their knees in an inability to move another fraction.

So many were influenced by the mead in the dark hours; Easter sunset had occurred some hours ago and the night was now inky black and quiet in hushed apprehension to events unfolding. The raucousness was entirely of a human sort; Mother Nature only observed from above. The pair below that most succumbed to the mead's influence were the two who were least able to afford the results.

The mead in its syrupy honeyed sweetness, so easy to drink, sip after many sips, warmed her insides as Catrione poured yet another goblet full of the golden liquid. The effects were beginning to overtake her as they heated her blood and brought a sense of dreaminess to her mind. She felt hot and her inhibitions were dissolving like the morning mists over the highlands when the noon day glow shined down.

She began to feel the drumbeats within her and the lower tones of the horns created a desire in her hips to shift instinctively in time to the beat. She swayed and her hips took on a life of their own; they circled and flowed in movement just as had the dancers who had entertained Cinaed earlier.

Atypically, Catrione and Cinaed were near one another; she standing and gently gyrating before him as he reclined before her. Cinaed brought his eyes up to Catrione and watched her as she began to dance a story for the ages, unfortunately.

Her hips were going to conquer. Her goal was exactly that!

Automatically, his cock roused in his inebriation; his flaring member continued to respond. Under his grimed, bloody and sweat dried battle tunic, Cinaed's cock was enlarging and lengthening in a rapid upward dance of its own. The alcohol and mindless expansion of his cock blended to shake him loose from any and all uncertainty that had lodged in his breast.

Catrione closed her eyes and felt the rhythm of the melodic sounds swirling about them. She moved dangerously close to Cinaed and leaned forward flirtatiously. She gave Cinaed an entire view of her cleavage while wiggling her dangling breasts in front of his face. The soft skin exposed was so touchable, Cinaed scarcely resisted. Catrione's rounded buttocks were raised and jutted out so exotically. Her smooth tight curves there were wondrous at her or anyone's age. Quickly, Cinaed ran a hand over one of them.

She held bells in her hands and the coins tied around her wrists clinked and jingled as she performed in her erotic fashion, drunkenly parading before Cinaed. The husband was gone and she was free, blessedly free. The mead continued to work its powerful magic as she subtly writhed ever closer and then met with this man's gaze. Oh those wondrous eyes of his.

Those eyes sent shivers spiking through her.

She kept with her hypnotic sway and now her fulsome breasts lingered enticingly in front of Cinaed. He lifted his head and his tongue darted out with pointed tip and flicked quickly over her firm, thick and elongated nipple. Her bounty there remained covered still but in a thin, diaphanous material that truly bared so many of her outsize details.

Catrione was empowered by the effect of the mead and the sensuality of his darting tongue. She had no further inhibitions at all and so wanted to lead him to an empty chamber. She stepped backwards, keeping her intense gaze poised upon him as Cinaed eagerly followed her; happy to clasp her hand and steady himself also.

The chamber was very dark, and Catrione and Cinaed learned quickly to see with their hands; the mead having blunted the usually powerful eyesight of a vampire. Catrione pulled him close to her and kissed him forthrightly. Their lips met, tongues soon followed, stirring up what fed their flame. Their kisses became feverish now and, as they kissed, Cinaed easily found Catrione's breasts. He stripped off the light covering material and her mounds swung to him. He cupped them and used his thumbs and index fingers to fan the heat more within her. She brought his head down to suckle there, thrusting her now unfettered breasts into his face and deeper into his avaricious mouth. His hot soft tongue tip lashed at her still swelling nipples. She moaned fervently.

The jewel between her legs was a radiant molten nugget of bronze now. She must have him! She begged him to jerk off his trews and reveal himself fully to her. He complied instantly and flung them aside. On the floor, Cinaed was fondling his large member. It was responding, huge and flaring. Catrione felt this and with her hand over his, passionately assisted him in stroking his throbbing shaft that she so desperately craved. The dew drop had formed and they both experienced the slickness of it as Catrione rubbed it all over the head of his cock.

She straddled him then and with one swift move took him fully into her.

Three long grinds down his shaft and then around and around in circular motion provided all the lubrication that the pumping required. Catrione rode up and down his length and felt his pelvis bounce against the mouth of her womb and exquisitely vibrate the jewel above.

She had known this feeling before and remembered it finely; bobbing up and down, up and down while he twisted and pulled at her sensitive nipples.

They must let this coupling come to a climax quickly in one motion. He slipped around to the top position and slid Catrione underneath him. She wrapped her legs around his waist as he started pounding into her. Harder and harder, faster and faster went his unrelenting strokes until miraculously, at the same moment, they erupted in an explosion of spurting come and unbridled spasms of pleasure released.

They clung together and the mead that had inspired them overtook them. They fell fast into a short lived, yet deep, slumber.

Catrione awakened as she sensed that the hour was about at hand for sunrise. She forced herself to full consciousness then. She touched the face next to hers. And this face seemed as if it was . . . . Cinaed's, her son! His lips were not the same as those that she had kissed so many times over. Ohh, that face! Ohh no! Hell's horrors, this is Cinaed!

Catrione jumped from him and then returned to shake Cinaed roughly. "What have we done?! Oh what have we done?! Cinaed awaken! Cinaed, awaken now! Oh this was an unfortunate mistake! Cinaed we have wronged! Please awaken!" She wailed and cried looking to the ceiling for aid and succor.

"We must leave here on the instant! We have been vile and have committed the most grievous sin imaginable!"

Cinaed was groggy yet. He revived himself enough to have recognized his mother's voice calling out to him. Suddenly he recognized the issue that they had entangled themselves within. He put his palm to her mouth in an effort to hush her and growled out, "We must never speak of this, do you understand?"

Catrione lamented in tears and vowed silence. "I will never talk about this transgression!" She also shook her head "no" as the tears persisted.

Cinaed rose quickly and pulled his trews up and about him, then they departed the chamber separately in order to disguise their act. He had defiled himself and his own mother! He departed her with this thought commanding his mind while his footsteps led him to Eumann and Catrione's nesting place. He was vampire now and required the same protection from the damnable fire of the sun as did Catrione. He appreciated that she was to follow closely upon his heels to hide from the toxic rays set to arrive in minutes.

She and Eumann, he was now mortal after having been released by the ancient vampire, were to share the tunnel. Cinaed was to burrow more deeply within and his mother and Eumann were to keep their abode in the forward portion of the earthen hole.

He entered there and heard her footsteps near to the opening that he had just entered. Both were spared the sun's ravages. He though had no intent of engaging with her again in conversation this day nor to ever again engage her as they had just done prior. This was his mother and he would respect their bond forever more!

Catrione had gathered her items and stolen from the chamber in the darkness. She had allowed for Cinaed to vanish from view and then she trailed him to safety. She whimpered softly for her love, Eumann, as she neared the entrance. Her eyes remained wet from so many tears.

Even the vampire within them both was ashamed and was aware of the abomination of their actions.

CHAPTER 22

Ashamed Consternation

It was a motley crew consisting of Catrione, Cinaed and Eumann. It was twelve hours later and Cinaed and Catrione were fully conscious. As the two vampires paced the tiny interior of their slightly rounded shelter, Eumann sensed a heightened tension between his paramour and her son. Eumann took a sizeable risk but queried in spite of that, "Catrione, Cinaed, is there something amiss between you both? You exude an energy that appears to clash decisively. And neither of you will glimpse the other. What is wrong between you two?"

Cinaed seemed angry in his agitation and Catrione seemed ashamed in her consternation. They were unable to sit still for more than brief seconds. Why they had stayed in each other's proximity when either or both could have darted out and away was confusing to Eumann.

Suddenly it occurred to him that they not only wished to reveal themselves to him but that they also had this kinetic vibration between themselves as if, perversely, they were strongly attracted and simultaneously despised and feared that attraction.

Eumann was planning on probing their very souls tonight!

"You and your mother, Cinaed, were absent from the feast for a period of time. What transpired with you in your absence? I need to know, I ought to know. Catrione, what was it?

I do love you Catrione and you may trust me with your most closely held secrets. Our love transcends anything that you could tell me here and now."

Cinaed was the first of the pair to reply though. "She enticed me and I will not allow it ever again!"

Eumann strode to where Catrione stood petrified and in place. He raised her eyes to his with the softest push of his fingers to her chin. She avoided his tender gaze and riveted her stare to the hard packed soil at her feet. Though she was vampire, she showed vivid and always honest emotions as she had pastime. To Eumann, that was priceless and meant more to him than any single incident could ever mean.

"Feel the sweetness in my gaze and in my touch of you my wonderful Catrione. There is nothing that can shatter our bond that you divulge to me. It is the act of enlightening me and honesty that performs the true binding for you and me. I must hear you now."

"Hear this tutor! You betrayed my father with my mother and my mother betrayed me in her evil luring of me to her. You and she are despicable and deserve the other. Yet she is blood and she loves you infinitely and profoundly.

For those reasons, I consent to have you, Eumann, and you, my mother, at my side in whatever the future may bring. But I will have you know in no uncertain terms that there is no other cause for my generosity and forgiveness with you.

And I will not remain here tonight a moment longer!" With that, Cinaed bolted from the tunnel and gusted from the exit out into the beckoning shadows.

Catrione raised her head at Cinaed's exit and replied in a hushed manner to Eumann, "He has changed since he returned without his father. He is so determined now to be strong beyond his years! It can only be a positive trait for him here on out.

As a vampire, I absolutely comprehend that what was within you is now within him and it is a fierce force that does attract me; but only to a degree. Yet that small degree was built into a pillar of passion by the effects of the mead in the moon's last cycle.

Honestly though, most of me believed that it was you whom I was engaging with when it was actually Cinaed. And I was stunned in the hour prior to dawn when I realized that it was not you. I felt a face then and gasped as I recognized my son next to me.

So yes, Cinaed and I coupled. It was tragic and will never be repeated. And if I could take back the singular incident I would, in an instant without a backward glance!

I love him but not in a way of intimacy. He is my son and that is all and enough!

Your gentleness, your loving empathy as the man that you have become since our last spent passion are the aspects of you that I so fully cherish. That you contain no vampire qualities any longer is of zero importance to me."

Eumann was held spellbound by her remonstrations and explanations. He also was aware that he was no longer leashed to the entity that had gripped his core. Additionally, Catrione's genuine expressions rubbed away any momentary jealousy, resentment or anger that he experienced due to Catrione and Cinaed's sexual exploits together.

He loved her still.

But he had to have answers related to possible issue; what the conceivable progeny of these two might he and she need to prepare for?

"Catrione, did I, as vampire, inform you of the method by which the undead may have children of their own? I ask because the matter of your potential pregnancy might loom large in the coming months and may force you into displaying your identity if you have a vampire for a child. That is simply guesswork but we must be ready for any and all outcomes.

Was there any kind of map laid out to you by me then in our casual conversations?

I hope to god that I did or that you discern the likelihood of descendants even if it was not explained to you by me!

Catrione was in Eumann's solid embrace presently and was stripped of her inhibitions and fears. The words expressed poured easily from her lips.

"You mentioned the mechanics of vampire birth. Since having been turned I realize it instinctively from the psychic gift of the undead.

A human male and vampire female may combine and she will have the capacity to give birth. An undead male and a human female may combine and again she also will have the proficiency to create a child.

Humans are necessary for vampires regarding their blood and their procreative skills.

In these situations, our fears can be lessened because most children of either union are not born vampire.

Cinaed and I cannot birth at all.

It is impossible for two vampires, male and female, to bring forth any being whatsoever."

Eumann sighed and his relief was palpable.

He kissed Catrione at the crown of her head to begin.

CHAPTER 23

Kilmarten Coronation

The succession coronation for Cinaed was in progress at Dunadd Hill Fort in county Kilmarten. It was spring and dusk had established itself hours ago. Cinaed had to be very chary of that and had his faithful, trusted, yet loathed tutor, Eumann, perform in his stead in the bright of day when he was not able. He also had a secret henchman whom he believed in fully to watch over Eumann. One could never have too many of those whom one relied upon without reserve.

This was why Cinaed had insisted upon an evening coronation. Though it was unusual, he was now the approaching titular head of Dal Riata after all and his commands were ultimately law.

Were it not for the primal strength of the undead entity within him he would have experienced a sensation of being overwhelmed at the process as it engulfed him.

This location, Dunadd Hill Fort, was chosen by prior kings as the formal and now traditional crowning place of the Gaelic kings. The village that offered a friendly perimeter for the castle itself was often regarded as the capitol of Dal Riata. Cinaed permitted that belief to remain in circulation amongst his people as he was so very fond of the village of

Lochgilphaed. The commoners here were his extended kith and kin and he loved them all dearly.

The fort itself was a fist of stone perched on the edge of Crinan Moss in Argyll. It made for the ideal defensive position as it was encircled by a flat mossy field at its base that gave view to any and all would be invaders. This moss also tended to collect moisture and any weight of man, horse or assault devices sank some and were therefore slowed or completely thwarted in any attack by that fact.

Cinaed was greatly impressed by those who had built this fortress and who had gone before him in establishing residence here. The fact that pride in his deceased and also fervently alive countrymen made him swell with large satisfaction. His Pictish remnant was constantly restrained and held at bay by him as his personal history had bent him away from that portion of his rich and glorious heritage.

As a final structural impediment to the enemy that Cinaed perceived, as he stood as God Almighty above the throngs below, was that the sides of the hill that the fort stood upon were terraced and nearly impossible to scale. Foes rarely attacked the Dal Riatans at this particular site. And when they were foolhardy enough to attempt an overthrow via this route, their challenge was indubitably cast back and they were routed in a manner that cost those adversaries plenty in the treasure of their lives and armaments.

Further particulars of the fort itself included the massive walls that Cinaed planted himself on at this very moment. As the occasional flurry of wind shot past him and his raiment was sometimes touched by the breeze, his thoughts ran to the fact that these bulwarks were each ten meters thick with a citadel mounted atop the structural monstrosities. They were impervious to onslaught and kept all within in a never faltering security.

Crowds were gathered below as they gleefully peered up to the imminent coronation of their newly established King Cinaed. Even in the dim shroud of midnight, Cinaed's silhouette shimmered visibly against the night sky as a full moon threw its illumination to the pageant from a cloudless black horizon. The regal aspect of the muscled and considerable form of Cinaed ensconced in a lush and stately robe with a gaudy gold crown over his perfectly fitting helmet, finely crafted scepter and flashing a superbly wrought and gleaming silver hued sword, he appeared powerful and, yea, ready to take any and all the reigns of this Gaelic Kingdom into his oversized clenched hands immediately.

The Christian bishop stood to one side of Cinaed and the Druid priest to his other side. It was one of those rare moments when the observation was of the ancient and pagan standing peacefully together in the vicinity of the godliness of the new religion which had and was sweeping the countryside in a wave of unstoppable fervent evangelizing by the spirit of Columba and the written gifts of the recently deceased Bede. The two spiritual adversaries, pagan and Christian, were never to join in union but just to be able to witness the simple and calm coexistence of the two in proximity was magnificent. And it was not to happen again as Cinaed easily discerned that a profound and permanent transition was upon them all as the old was about to yield to the tide of the fresh and the golden. It was cataclysmic and was to take not only his culture by storm; the world was to feel the effects of this phenomenon.

The masses gathered at a distance were neither privy to the words passed by Druid to the pending King nor to the words shared by Christian representative to Cinaed either.

And that was even as the fascinated bodies below were hushed and rapt in the grandeur of this instant.

They perceived the motions and observed the sign of the cross made by the Christian. Both priest and bishop leaned in and kissed Cinaed's right and left cheek simultaneously. To the impatient throng, that was enough to signify that their man, Cinaed, had been officially installed as their overlord, their leader and their king.

Cinaed warmed to his eager and captivated subjects. But he waited for the priest and bishop to step away from him. He had one more rite of passage to perform before his kingship was completely affirmed. The rowdy crowd knew this but was prepared to call Cinaed king early or late in the formalities in their joyous frenzy. They loved him and did not see the point for all of the pomp and circumstance required.

On the slope, near to the hill's summit, there were two rocks. The primary slab had a human footprint and a basin carved into its surface.

Without assistance or accompaniment now, Cinaed walked placidly and smoothly to that rock. It was only when he set his own foot into that footstone that he became married to the land that he ruled. And so he removed his shoe from his foot and placed that bare foot in the basin's pure water. Then, and only then, did he drop that cleansed foot into the carved imprint. He officially began his reign as both servant and master to the Dal Riatan land then.

The triumphal roar of the legion of people sounded in full chorus in that moment.

He was smote with a delighted gladness that was nearly unbearable in its overflow. He glanced at the secondary slab of stone and viewed momentarily the image of a wild boar stamped into its surface. The Ogam inscription there spoke volumes in its simplicity of the righteousness and responsibility of those who laid their fitted flesh into that imprint that always existed upon that oh so significant first stone.

The inscription on the second was an oath that Cinaed had just sworn to keep. He was honored and was certain of his successful completion of that oath in the unwinding of his forthcoming days.

Cinaed flashed his smile to his beaming public and hoisted his scepter and sword into the air over and over. As he did this the din of his people escalated and the satisfaction in their kingdom was sensed throughout the land.

It drifted to the territories of his foes as well.

Some sadness remained within Cinaed as he recollected that this occasion occurred because his father had suffered the misfortune of an arrogant man. Though Cinaed recognized this fact, he valued his father's capacity to persuade his warriors to obey him based upon his own determination and courage that he demonstrated on the battlefield each and every time he and his soldiers forayed out into conflict. To the vampire-Cinaed, arrogance was a requirement for the success of a great king. With arrogance went confidence. These twin traits brought valorous deeds and outcomes that ceded themselves into the grand hall of history. Cinaed saw his father's flaws as strength and he was not about to depart from this vision of the man whom he loved and cherished long after his father's death; he presumed at his own demise, he would still be in awe of his father's character and in the accomplishments that he carried to fruition.

Cinaed's grief clung to him but he was not at its mercy. He had nearly died twice and he had been cognizant in those episodes that, if he survived, he would forever be strong and fulfill a destiny that would not take him into emotional terrain. He would do whatever was required and use his connection with his father to conquer rather than to falter.

Sadness was weakness and he did not plan to permit his thoughts of his father to lessen him.

He was to only let it elevate him.

With that thought upon his brow, he finished with his salute to his people and marched to and through the gates of the fort.

All that his people saw was the dominant stride of a King who was indomitable and ever capable of arousing pride and a desire for victory inside their hearts.

CHAPTER 24

Dungeon's Paradise

They were relieved to have ample space and stone surroundings instead of the earthen hideout that they had gradually adapted to and grew accustomed with in their earlier days. Their relief related to the many fine and previously unused rooms that they had searched out and found in this magnificent fortress that they now called home. Dunadd Hill Fort was perfect for the vampire princess and her now completely human consort, Eumann.

That Eumann had been informed he was capable of impregnating Catrione aroused his confidence in that he had not already fathered a child with her. He did not understand the mechanics but had no longing or intention of having a child with Catrione or anyone ever. In their particular case, he cherished their bond and needed no other to enter it. That she had not conceived with him over the years, human, vampire or inhabited, must signify that they were to play indefinitely without that worry.

Catrione led him through the labyrinthine hallways of the fort's lowest level. She did not require any candle. He did as he saw only with weakened human eyes and so he carried several beeswax candles with him.

He wanted undead powers back. He wanted to walk as proudly as she walked now. And he had given her those powers in addition. He planned on an insistence in this regard as he and Catrione dallied. If it came to barter, he was willing to do that too.

Her mood was one of rippling eagerness and excitement as she forged ahead of Eumann.

She internally observed Cinaed's concentrated focus on her and she returned the favor all the while fully intending to cavort just with Eumann. It did give her vanity a prick of pleasure to discern her influence not over Cinaed but her prior vampire lover. She thrilled to that notion and it pleased her no end. Yet she was never about to entwine with her own son again!

She almost hissed in delight as she pushed a thick and wooden door open. As it fell inward, it disappeared from sight. The veil of darkness inside this area blocked vision to all of its objects except to her.

He chuckled as Catrione pointed out the items that incited her so readily. Visualization was not required as in her gusto she managed to summarize each and every piece of furniture and other therein. As she trilled through the pieces, his vision began to adjust and he was cognizant of most all that stood before them.

"Eumann, this had to have been a room of torture or imprisonment at some previous time! Here is a long wooden table that must have been used to tie down individuals and subject them to torment until they gave in. In this dungeon there are also several leather stranded whips and leather bands for restricting the movement of wrists and ankles. The table has holes bored into it at its head, center and foot. And do you see the belts attached to those holes? Strong and thick leather they are. There is a hinge at three quarters length as well. That must have been to use when the torturer dropped the table at that point in order to stretch the captives belly and increase the pain.

This shows so much intricacy in the methods of retrieving information from unwilling adversaries!"

Eumann was overwhelmed by the myriad of instruments and contraptions in such a small space. The table's length spanned the entire room.

"This shall be our play room upon occasion as Cinaed has provided us with our own sleeping chamber already. The hearth, the bed, the two sarcophagi are all that we need there. And it is lush in comparison with what we had prior.

But this room has my complete attention for the moment."

Catrione removed her tunic then without waiting upon Eumann's request or involvement. Her belted and sheathed full breasts cascaded from her garments. All else was removed rapidly as Eumann froze in lust at her erotic antics, though it was nothing more than the revelation of her unclothed body. The strength of his response to the simplicity of her action meant that he was hers profoundly.

In a trice, she raised her petit bottom up onto the table surface and immediately flattened herself to it and extended her arms to the table top.

"Take me my lovely man." Her smile fanned across her face.

His heart beat fiercely but he had to broach the subject now! "Catrione, I will do your tiniest bidding tonight but I have my own request of you. I do not wish to remain human. I have to be vampire again. Do that for me and I am your slave forever."

She did not miss an instant as she answered, "I planned that for you and for you and me always. I cannot be without you. So you will always be mine throughout eternity as undead together. I offer that gift to you gladly and freely.

Now honor my desires here and now.

Buckle my wrists and ankles to the table. Fasten them tightly as I want to know that my restraints are firm and challenge my freedom without doubt."

Eumann placed the candle holder and flickering candles down upon the floors surface. He needed the light no more. And then he stepped over to Catrione and the table and buckled her to it hard. He was now as eager as she was. Yet he was equally cognizant of the fact that this was an offering of restrained pain and captivity only to heighten their passion. Any serious roughness was to be resisted. Catrione would not allow it anyhow unless she so desired exactly that.

Catrione's mounded chest rose to sweet heights as she lay there. Her nipples beckoned but he was going to await her instructions before he made further moves. His cock grew as he examined her lines. She had beautiful flowing hair, gorgeous heart shaped face, very plentiful breasts, exceptionally so, a sweep from there to just faintly curved belly and then a quick slope to her Venus mound and vault and finally to sleek and slender legs. She was delectable and she was his. Now he was ready to hear her every demand.

"Walk to me and stand behind me," she ordered. He followed through with this. He then leaned over her and kissed her sweet and full lips swiftly. This upside down kiss stirred them both. As he pressed his lips to hers, he grasped her thick brown nipples and pulled and twisted them with increasing strength. Catrione sighed and then moaned that this was perfect.

He had been given a handful of cut threads by her before they had even left their sleeping chambers in search of dungeon level paradise. She had advised him what she wanted with that innocent appearing material. So he performed upon her prior directions now. He was no longer kissing her nor toying with her nipples. Instead, he tied lengths of thread around each nipple. He tightened them just enough to cause constriction, a sensation of pain and greater engorgement of blood within her hot buds.

In his momentary change of position, he also removed a feather, such a surprise for his love, from a pocketed fold in his tunic and traced that from her neck over her breasts and passion-thudding nipples in a straight line down to her navel. He did not run it over her nether region as he desired her anticipation to build and flame from the teasing above her waist first. He put the feather down and could not resist kneading her wondrous pale colored soft risen bosom. That flesh of hers being gently massaged caused her to squirm her hips slightly and breathe a bit faster and deeper. He was unable to resist pinching and twisting her bulbous nipples again. She writhed for the moments that he did this and panted in the pleasure of his touch there. The intense burn in her tips was so powerful to her as she lay upon the table.

Instants after elevating her heat in this manner, he reached for one of the leather tasseled small whips available. He dragged the ends of these tassels over her zaffre shaded visible veins flowing to her contracted aureoles. She whispered "yessss" under her breath then.

He broke away from her fractionally and snapped the whip in the air. He did this at her side and none of the leather strands touched her. She startled though and panted harder anticipating further unknown approaches by Eumann. And what he did next was to drag those leather strands over her belly in repeated circles. Again, he stepped back and snapped the strands into making a sharp striking sound. Catrione was unable to hold her hips still and they alternated between rotation and elevation. Her nether lips glistened as well.

Eumann had to bite her straining and swollen nipples with the edges of his teeth. He did it hard enough that she cried out in that burn that she so sought and loved.

His cock was huge by now. His side vein pulsed and his shaft was thick and long, his cockhead dripping and plum sized. He spread her nether lips and licked the entire gleaming area once. Her hips jerked and she gasped.

He squeezed her large swollen ruby clit between thumb and forefinger gently and repeatedly. That miniscule action seemed to work incredible magic on Catrione who trembled like a leaf and moaned deeply. He then sucked her in and lashed his tongue upon her throbbing marble. Its delectable smoothness magnetized him to it.

She rasped out these words next, "Get the candle and use it. Now!"

The beeswax had melted into a syrupy gelatinous hot mix and he poured a tiny trail of it from between her breasts to her Venus vault's opening. She groaned, "Ohhhhhhhhh ummmmmm."

He slid his trews off and stroked his member tightly and rapidly. His legs shivered and weakened as he stroked in an ever more rapid rhythm on himself. Catrione was panting hard and fast now and was writhing on the wood surface.

The table's hinge was placed exactly at the juncture of her spread legs. He first released the belts from her ankles and held her vibrating legs in his powerful hands. He leaned forward and triggered the hinge so that the lower panel of the table dropped to a ninety degree angle. This assured him easy access to her opening.

He pointed his cock to her. First though, he bent to her throbbing jewel and bit it firmly but without excess pressure. Catrione jerked and felt her wrist restraints begin to give. Her clit was massive and almost purple in shade.

She pleaded with him, "Enter me. Oh my god, enter me this instant."

He did not and requested that she beg for his rod again.

She lifted her hips upward and cried, "I have to have you. Oh please Eumann, place it in me. Please my love, please!" She nearly snarled that as she was so fraught with passion.

He stained her lips with his copious clear dew and then was not able to keep from sheathing himself within her. He had no more control and pounded her with his length hard, deep and in a blur. His pelvis hammered hers and her jewel vibrated from his repeated impact. He had her ankles wedged over his shoulders and she raised her hips to him and stroked him as he stroked her.

She tore through her wrist bonds then and raked her nails over his chest. Then in a paroxysm of heat took his nipples and gripped them so firmly. He tremored and approached his threshold. She knew that and was balanced at the edge of the cliff of her want as well.

He growled his release and shot copious loads of pearly white ejaculate into her. Her hips were driven skyward and her shoulders and head came involuntarily forward. Her vault was engulfed in wave after wave of intense release. It was huge and she was carried on its high crest.

It was at this moment that she lanced his neck and delivered her gift to him.

CHAPTER 25

Doors Wide Open

It had been five years since the Pictish King Oengus II had given himself in conflict as he opposed Cinaed's father and Cinaed. Cinaed, since not the king of two joined regions, Gael and Pict, had to be content as king of only Dal Riata. His ambition was greater than to lead Dal Riata alone but that ambition was in its fledgling stages and was only to advance as opportunity dictated.

The Pictish inheritor after Oengus II was that of Uven Mac Angus and Cinaed sensed through those undead powers of his that the Pictish land was about to be enveloped in utmost crisis if that was not occurring in this instant. It was not Cinaed or his followers who were delivering misery and destruction to the territory of the northeastern most British Isles.

The Vikings of Denmark, principally, stormed over Cinaed's neighbors after they had proclaimed offshore islands as their own. From these bastions of hell for the Picts, the brutal Scandinavians made their frequent forays into mainland provinces; and those provinces were held at a huge cost of Pictish life and limb. These Nordic warriors arrived for the plunder and booty. They relished the carnal freedom that they had with the women whose men they had just killed. They seemed to favor the application of carnage to the land and the people who fell before their sword; if, in the process, they were capable of holding the communities under their dominion, so much the better.

The Pictish population had been severely damaged in the conflagration that had occurred between themselves and the Gaels. And now they were being savaged from a different flank by a very recent enemy that was ferocious, without regard for mercy and who overcame almost anyone who had the misfortune to stand before them.

Cinaed was pleased that it was Catrione's people who had to deal with this tide of battle against madmen.

He and his fellow Dal Riatans were not threatened as the Pictish were from the Dane's offshore incursions. The Dal Riatan neighbors were Irish Gaels whose ancestors had actually populated the land for Cinaed and his citizenry. Ireland and Dal Riata were brethren joined in an alliance that was born of blood relations and neither group permitted anyone to strike violently at one or the other. To see eye to eye with surrounding folk was to allow one's kingdom to prosper without hindrance. He had this advantage. The Pictish nation did not. And they were suffering intensively for it.

Uven Mac Angus and his brother Bran as well as the plentiful Pictish nobility were in a devastating war with the ship-riding renegades and it had gathered into a fever pitch toward resolution. Cinaed observed the ebb and flow of their skirmishes and then their larger encounters also. Both had mounted in frequency and aggressiveness and he discerned that one vast, collective struggle was nigh.

Cinaed was without an ability to visualize how this conflict was to end. The outcome, as all future events for Cinaed were yet thus, remained shrouded in dense veils of greys, blacks and whites that shielded the truth of those events from him. He was aggrieved at this limitation but was practicing the undead art and was finding his vision to be ever strengthening.

What Cinaed hoped for especially was that there would be mass slaughter on both sides and that he could then bring the land easily to his breast. That served him and Dal Riata the best as strife and loss of Dal Riatan life would be minimized and possibly not occur at all. That was his fervent first wish. He presumed that he was not about to find himself that fortunate.

His next inclination was that the Pictish slay the ruthless Vikings with little Pictish power left to resist his own invasion then. And besides, the frightening capacity of the Vikings would not have to be dealt with in that case. But Cinaed had little faith in the Pictish facility to conquer the strange and seemingly invincible soldiers from shores that were as a lightning bolt to this land.

Another thought was that the Vikings, once they had purloined plenty of plunder from homes, churches and from the corpses of the slain, would find satisfaction and simply sail off and disappear forever into the embrace of horizon's arms. Cinaed burst out in hardy laughter upon this imagining. What fantasy he was engaging in. These men were here to stay and the clarity of that fact was so obvious.

Finally, he chose this last as the probable outcome as it had the ring of reality all about it. The two cultures would find a fitful finish in their warfare and the Vikings would retreat to their taken lands and the Pictish would maintain theirs. Cinaed would either have to fight the Pictish for their throne or find a claim to that throne that sold itself to one and all.

Cinaed waited with bated breath as events happened that were not within his control. And he lusted for control. So, in spite of his tension, he waited with everyone else who waited.

The suspense was short in its existence and the conclusion of fists to face and weapons to bodies was seen by Cinaed.

It was neither the worst nor the best that confronted him. He coveted the Pictish throne. But it was not to find its way to him smoothly. So what had transpired between the rival hoards?

The Picts had not been vanquished. Yet many of these tattooed rivals had been laid low in death. King Uven Mac Angus and his brother Bran had been finished off. Notable Pictish lords had been sent to their deaths as well. The Pictish royalty had been decimated and there was harsh question as to the legitimate next successor. And, Cinaed pondered, who might want that crown as the people were reduced in rank heavily and the land lay in much ruin?

He sought that crown still and saw the advantages of a united Alba under him. And he was a very determined man.

The Vikings had lost their interest in assuming control over the Pictish territory. It appeared that booty was the primary motivation there. Once they had picked the pockets clean of their adversary, they left back to the shelter of their island dens.

And that was fortunate for Cinaed as he had contemplated having to take a defensive posture against the Vikings as they came to his lands in search of further booty. Their craving had somehow been sated though and Cinaed was not at risk of expending men and arms in an entrenched war with them.

His days of unending bloodlust were, thankfully, being more and more assuaged by increasingly benign impulses that sometimes mystified him while at other times satisfied him.

What he was privy to was that he was now a claimant, without having to resort to a clash of arms, in his own right for the title over Pictland. The doors had opened wide in his pursuit of expansion of his rule. He was also privy to the knowledge that he was to have opposition and probably a stubborn and benighted opposition at that.

His mother was of value to him at long last. She had disappointed him repeatedly and he had almost left her to fend for herself once he had taken power over Dal Riata. He had relented somewhat and had also given her lover, Eumann, freedom to closet himself with Catrione. He had given her the right to roam within the castle and stand at Cinaed's side as he arrived at ceremonies and pronounced edicts.

She would step aside once he discovered his queen.

She was not to be banished then but she was to find herself and Eumann marginalized and stripped of most any power in that moment.

He looked to that moment eagerly and thought of Aiobheean often in that regard.

His yearnings for Aiobheean were to push his ambivalent sentiments towards his mother into an oblivion that would still that desire he felt for Catrione.

CHAPTER 26

Naked Greed

That they stubbornly refused to accept his bona fides for the Pictish kingship, once Uven and Bran were buried in the ground, caused him consternation and a grave displeasure. His intellect, this time, played to the vampire within while his emotions played to the frailer human within. The demon aspect of Cinaed readily understood the resistance of Cinaed's opposition, his challengers. They sought power as Cinaed sought it. There was no rational or logical impetus other than the naked greed of fulfillment of needs for domination. How well his beast inside recognized that motivation. Yet Cinaed's human segment, which prevailed only rarely, demanded that a list of logical factors laid out before them ought to predominate over all else. Scrupulous logic before emotion was how a man was supposed to behave, was it not? Damn them that they did not yield and conform to his most compelling wishes.

In his mind, he ticked off the items that irrevocably indicated his entitlement to the lands from which his mother came. Surely they were to reasonably surrender to him soon enough. They must do that eventually he insisted to himself.

He was not ordinarily patient whatsoever but was willing to allow some small amount of time to pass for clarity to sink into their hides and minds. The clarity, after all, was so vivid and vibrant! To him, all reasonable men disputing his rights there would immediately set aside their issues once apprised of the information that he had in his possession. Were his adversaries to take a simple moment to do their own reflecting on the matter that would surely persuade them to instantly withdraw their own claims and cease doubting his?

The most obvious claim had, at its source, the fact that his mother was a Pictish princess of the Royal House of Fortrenn. No one disputed that her blood flowed through his. And by the rule of Pictish culture itself; the kingdom was passed via the lineage of the woman, his mother, Catrione. Oddly though, the female determined who was to be lord and master in Pictland yet it was only the male who became king. She bestowed her royal lineage upon him and he, therefore, rightfully planned on making his application for the Pict's highest seat based upon that well established fact.

That alone served him mightily in his argument for seating himself in the now involuntarily vacated throne. He was Catrione's son; so he stood above all others as his assertion in this matter was far superior and could not be challenged rationally.

Other righteous factors for this petition piled up and added thorough solidity to what he knew belonged only to him.

Were they blind to the fact that he was of the mighty clan Gabhran? This clan had produced a majority of capable kings in the wider area of this northern region. They were his ancestors; his father, King Alpin Mac Eachaidh, was prominent amongst these hallowed names. There was also King Aedan Mac Gabhran and King Mael Colium Mac

Donnchada who performed wondrous acts on behalf of the greater locality.

And, as kings go, his great grand uncle had sown the seeds for unifying Dal Riata and Pictland forever as both had been governed under his hand. But then he had been deposed by the cunning and conniving Oengus I and the lands were divided once again.

Was this not enough to convince rival Pictish nobles? It seemed not; not yet.

It suddenly occurred to him how differently the two sectors, Dal Riata and Pictland, though they were neighbors, had settled upon such diametrically opposed methods of choosing their kings.

As he had included in his case for the Pictish throne, women were primary in how Pictish leaders were selected. The brothers, the sons, the relatives of the queen or princess were the candidates for high position. The women were the lynchpin for the men in their progression into ultimate authority.

But in Dal Riata, women were nonessential in picking those viable to lead. The father was followed in sequence by his eldest son, or first son in whichever birth position or any male of blood surrounding whomever was the present sovereign.

Women never controlled the kingdom in either system.

In Pictland, at least, a woman experienced empowerment that a woman in Dal Riata did not. To have some impact upon significant political events was a taste at least.

It was a taste that Cinaed did not wish to encourage. His mother's lineage assisted him in his stake for expansion of territory for himself, yes, most definitely. That was well and good as it served his purposes. He was not even remotely inclined to serve hers. He was not about to have a woman usurp privileges or authority ever. It was a dangerous route if one gave reins to a female for the very reason of this: even if she was capable of handling those reins, a very unlikely possibility, would she ever return them to the stupid male who had ceded his power to her?

He ceased his ruminations here as it was folly to continue in this vein of thought. It was a world for and controlled by men! What had the Picts intended when they had established such a bizarre route to leadership? If he never found himself King of Pictland and never asserted his ways regarding his hope for their ultimate demise, he was certain that the Pictish culture would vanish anyhow as the involvement of women in any way, shape or form over a territories fate was a weakness that could never be overcome.

He was unable to resist wondering how his precious Aiobheean might react to his mode of thinking.

She was a very special woman he knew. Yet she was not foolhardy enough to desire breeching the outer margins of established convention. She had had child and was most certainly tending to her nurture of raising that child in a manner most feasible for success. She may have found a partner and spouse and maintained the kitchen and hearth of their wheelhouse. Whatever path she had taken, she was not involved in any rebellious actions or behavior contrary to God's law for women.

Columba and Bede had waxed eloquent regarding the station that a woman must place herself in and to whom she owed her entire allegiance. She owed that to her male counterpart as he hunted, warred, ruled and took her to his bed when he required.

He was largely his father's son.

As he paced the floors and hallways of his stony royal abode, he took sight of Eumann as Eumann approached him.

Cinaed had dismissed his bodyguards as he liked to stroll through the intricate passages of his fortress alone. It gave his restless spirit periods where he was able to console himself on his own.

Eumann was cognizant of Cinaed's habit but found it disturbing. Though there was always some tension between the two, Eumann saw the strength of the man before him and did not ever chose to find him careless and then slain because of that.

"May I find you your way back to the King's chamber, Ma lord?" Eumann replied as he stopped and faced Cinaed.

It annoyed Cinaed immensely that Eumann was trying to abridge his freedom. So he replied, "You may not. I can find my own way there . . . . when I want to return to that location!"

"Yes, Ma lord." Eumann fumed that his thought to protect his liege lord was so easily rebuffed.

Would the two ever settle their differences?

CHAPTER 27

The Four Conspirators

It was as if his higher power was permitting him to visualize the present thoughts and actions of these four Pictish lords in particular and with a clarity that he was not usually able to muster. Their plans and conspiracies against him demonstrated to Cinaed that they were his deep antagonists and foes. They plotted for possession of what was rightfully his alone!

Cinaed was so attached to his notion of empire building and his notion of control of Pictland and Dal Riata, the fantastical combination thereof called Alba in his Gaelic tongue, that his obsessions with his lost and tender love, Aiobheean, were dimmed and nearly cast out. But his subterranean synapses were actually forever branded by her and would not ever truly release her image.

What names did these four riders of his apocalypse go by? The names were foul to Cinaed and their appellations were Brude Mac Ferat, Kynat Mac Ferat, Bruide Mac Fotel and most lethal yet simultaneously naïve and gullible at times was Drust IX Mac Ferat. The latter was the youngest but very sly and cunning.

Cinaed seethed and planted seeds for their overthrow and vanquishing in these moments of a frosted winter's eve in the year of eight forty one. It had been seven annual cycles since he had been crowned King of the Dal Riatan realm. He was in his prime now at age thirty.

His realm thrived in this time of peaceful prosperity for his kinsmen. But he was itching for more.

All the while his Pictish neighbors continued to barely regrow from the disastrous effects upon them of the wars of eight thirty four and of eight thirty nine. The Picts were presently left alone by both Cinaed's people and by the Vikings.

Cinaed surmised that he had to establish his claim soon, whether through resort to arms, treachery or persuasive diplomacy.

The Pictish lords sustained their growth and building strength as no adversaries sought their door. That was Cinaed's cause for alarm and recognition that a plan to intervene and take over the Pictish crown had to be forged as soon as possible.

Fortunately for Cinaed, there was periodic strife and dissension that transpired between the significant lords aforementioned. That pattern of powerful disagreement usually followed family lines. The three sons of Ferat, Brude, Kynat and Drust IX were at odds, when tempers flared, with the son of Fotel, Bruide.

These moments of discord amongst the four lay principally with thoughts and strategies for rendering Cinaed harmless; and, completely separate from this issue was the question of whom now and, if necessary, who needed follow in order to reign supreme in Pictland. The three brothers and Bruide all clamored for leadership. And they aired this desire frequently between themselves.

Their thinking went thus: setting aside the matter of Cinaed briefly, they were to share power as a quadrumvirate, or each was to lead for an equal span of years until all four had led and then move through that rotation again or the conventional, which was to present a dominant assertion of rights; or, most obviously, they had the option of simply battling one another for the privilege.

It was almost a foregone conclusion that the more civil approaches would have short lived considerations. These, after all, were men of passion, temper and a high regard for brute and naked strength. The high road was sure to be overlooked from this breed of men.

So what did that leave them? Cinaed knew. It left them the conventional tactic. That meant that a supreme claim must be shown or supreme brawn must be shown. The former was impossible as no one of these four had superior lineage or any other entitlement. And were they to come to blows, the three Ferat sons would most likely clash with the Fotel son.

This outcome was only headed off by their overarching fear of Cinaed the interloper. If they fought between themselves, they became instantly weakened and were consequently vulnerable to attack from Dal Riata. So a tense and ongoing standoff loomed over the four lords. Time did nothing but solidify this circumstance. All were frustrated.

Strangely, the informal blueprint for leadership over this frame of time fell to Drust IX as he reflected a bold capacity that the others did not enjoy. The three others generally deferred to Drust. And his powers were plenty as three primitive men rarely yielded to their younger.

And then there was Wrad. He was a Pictish warrior who was independent of the four. His cohort may have been of the rabble and lesser ranks of the military but were, nonetheless, very dedicated to this consummately skilled and rebellious soldier. But Cinaed ignored Wrad as inconsequential and sent no messages to him.

Cinaed pieced it all together and presumed that he had to act abruptly and that it would have to involve treachery of the highest order. He was adept in that regard and assured himself of a method shortly.

His mother rarely visited him in his chambers but she had suddenly swept through to his lavish and royal bedroom.

What of this Cinaed speculated? His mother had avoided impropriety between them as had he since their unfortunate escapade in one another's arms. He recollected that embrace and it fired his soul quickly. She and Aiobheean had been his only intimate partners. They had spoiled him intensively by their wonderful bodies and lush responses. He imagined all other lovers to pale in the comparison. So he refrained. Yet here she was, and in his bedchambers no less.

Cinaed looked askance at her and then summarily waved his royal entourage away. They departed in the instant as he brooked no disregard when he required his way. And his way immediately was that he and she be alone. He chose to have all ears and eyes be absent for whatever was about to happen here and now. It might very well be innocent in nature but it very easily might be otherwise.

Catrione wore delicious raiment and all her lustrous beauty was attested to by the bold curves of clothing's material that clung to her in an hourglass configuration.

Cinaed was a King now and was not about to let his libido dictate to him this occasion.

"I have not visited you for so long my sweet son."

Cinaed was suspicious of her motives but actually had a question to ask her. "Mother, as you can see, I have but my trews on for the moment. I would have been more formally attired for you if I had known of your arrival."

She feigned a demure look and smiled. "Ask me whatever you wish."

"I am contemplating warfare again. It is possibly a very opportune interval for enlarging our domain.

I want to know that I am physically ready. I believe that I am but I want your opinion also. I will stand here and you tell me your reaction to my question."

What Catrione observed was of a man developed into a warrior's warrior. Cinaed's hair was very long and his auburn plaits hung thickly. He possessed a very bushy mustache that swooped downward, was a dark brown and had bursts of auburn highlight. His eyes were heavy lidded and his irises were the color of dark ale with cinnamon undertones. It was plain to observe that his arms and legs were muscular with those muscles defined and sinewy. Even in his almost nonexistent attire, he wore thick metal silver hued bracelets and leather thong braids tied around his bulging biceps. She also noticed that the tip of his cock appeared at the lower edge of his flaxen shorts. It was wide and round even in its semi slumber with slight momentary arousal. She reflected upon his thick and long size and the bluish vein that bulged and throbbed under her ministrations. She believed that his erection functioned as well now as then.

But she had not emerged here to seduce her son. That was a once and only happening.

What she said to him was, "You are most assuredly ready and equipped for battle. Do not worry that."

She moved forward to him and reached for his cock then. She let it stir within her grasp. She even rubbed his dew around his expanding cockhead. Of a sudden, she released him and they both stepped away from the other.

"I desired letting you know that, even in the most intimate of situations, I am able to resist our entwining."

He spoke immediately in reply, "I would have not allowed it to happen were you to have carried it further."

She stared his way for but an instant, turned rapidly and strode from the area.

CHAPTER 28

Lusty Inclinations

Cinaed was in his castle. It was eventide, but for Cinaed, the morning of his undead day. He had been washed, dressed and cared for by the maids. He was wide awake. Fortunately he considered, not every moonlit night was set for a battle.

He felt a stirring in his loins for some kind of pleasure seeking. He filled a goblet with mead. At first sip, the honey sweet liquid rolled down his throat. A sip became a gulp and the goblet of saffron liquid was gone in no time. Cinaed poured himself another and carried it with him as he ambled through the darkened halls in his grand stone home.

In his wandering, Cinaed spied a fragment of light being emitted from a room further down. His curiosity was pricked and he strode toward the illumination. The maids and the servants resided there. It was his castle and he had royal right to be anywhere inside that he chose.

Nearing this room, Cinaed noticed the door was opened enough to observe the unwitting entertainment inside. Two of his chamber maids were readying for bed and were engaged in a grooming session.

Both were young women of nubile beauty. Did he even know their names? Peigi, the one who appeared slightly older, looked freshly scrubbed with cheeks of soft rose pink. She was of slimmer build and he noticed her breasts thrusting high yet jutting out only so far. Her hips were narrower, yet well-defined above her long legs. Her hair was long, straight, light brown and naturally tipped with blonde at the ends. Her eyes were large, round and of a bold brown, and he was able to see her long eyelashes from where he stood. She reminded him of a doe.

The younger lass, Jinti, paired in a very complimentary manner with Peigi's appearance. Jinti was rounder and softer in aspect. Her long tightly curled auburn hair draped over her back. He imagined that her larger breasts were pendulous under her clothing and that her nipples would be stained a blackberry color. Her belly was round and sat above lushly ample hips. She was freckled and her innocent green eyes sparkled from across the room.

Cinaed sipped on the mead and contemplated entering the room. He decided the best place for him was to be in the dark of the hallway. He was very much enjoying their sweet collaboration.

On the table there was a flask of mead that one of these mischievous lasses had hidden in a tunic. Each of them was sipping the nectar of honey from the flask directly and were passing it back and forth happily.

Peigi was behind Jinti, brushing her auburn locks. They were being playful and speaking in tones that suggested that they pretended to be of high born status. Cinaed heard them sharing secrets about himself! Peigi reflected, "Our King is so muscular and of such strength and rugged handsome looks!" Jinti feigned a swoon, "Oh, would that I could lie in his arms! What would that feel like?!"

"Mmm, the mead is warming".

Jinti turned her head to face Peigi and confided "I have never known a man. Have you experienced the intimacy that can be shared between a man and a woman?"

Peigi quieted Jinti, her cheeks flushed some, and brushing a hand across Jinti's arm replied, "I have known the pleasure of being with a man or two, dear friend, and it is wicked and wicked pleasure! Shhh! I must hush speaking of such things". Peigi giggled then and gave Jinti's hair a soft pull.

"Ouch! Oh, 'ey, share with me now! I must know how to love a man! Tell me! Share with me! My time of learning is this moment! What if I were to be with my lover tomorrow? I must grasp what to do! Whisper to me, please! Share every secret with me!

I have kissed my own hand in practice, but it does not respond with kisses back" Jinti was nearly whining as she pleaded with Peigi to help her with this knowledge. Jinti took a big gulp of the mead, and was instantly transported to a cozier spot in her mind.

Cinaed's ears pricked up and they hastened to the words approaching as he wanted to hear answers from the teacher, Peigi, herself. He settled into a comfortable location where the lasses were visible and he might acquire new insight this night. His cock stiffened under his trews. He patted himself there and by that assured his hidden friend that his inclusion was a given.

Peigi used words to describe very succinctly the act of coupling and how it was done. Jinti appeared incredulous and fearful of the very act. Her eyes were wide open and not blinking. "What are you saying?! That does not sound in the least bit to be of wicked pleasure!"

Shaking her head and laughing, Peigi decided to really give Jinti a hands on lesson in loving. "Come young one, do you even know what your body looks like?! I am going to show you the richness and wickedness of it all. Take off your tunic now, and we shall start with a bit of knowledge right here".

Jinti's eyes were still enormous, but the mead influenced her enough to think, why not! Both lasses removed their tunics and sat facing one another on the feather filled bed.

Cinaed's eyes focused hard as he took in a large gulp of the mead. He kept himself from even sighing, as he watched.

His cock grew more, enlarging in his trews. It was beyond Cinaed's influence at this point and he loosened his trews and held his hand to his member, stroking it gently.

Peigi continued to instruct Jinti. "See how we are the same yet so different? Touch your breasts and close your eyes. What do you feel? Use your palms; use your fingers. See how the slightest touch makes your nipples become tight and hardened. Does that feel pleasurable to you?

Now, pinch them, gently at first, then as hard as you can stand it. Do you enjoy the little bit of pain with the pleasure?" Peigi rolled her own nipples in her fingers and pulled on them, elongating them and watching them darken in color. She was feeling the pleasure of this herself and wanted to engage Jinti in a full episode. More of that sweet honeyed mead was necessary again to relax Jinti even further.

"There are other parts made just for pleasure my friend. Lean back and open your legs. Look at me. Have you ever seen your own body down there? Now you must!" Jinti made a comical face and wondered to herself in her innocence what she might find if she were to do as Peigi instructed.

Peigi insisted that Jinti feel the hair that covered the most precious area of delight. She took Jinti's hand and put it on her own fur covered mound. "Mine here is soft and thick. Now feel your own, curly and bushy. We are so different, yet so uniquely made. Open yourself down there and look for the treasure. You will find a button that houses the very center of your pleasure. It exists for nothing else but that. See it, but don't touch it, not yet".

Jinti looked at Peigi's nether parts and saw the button there, tiny and smooth and very red. She looked down at herself and saw her own knob of bliss larger than Peigi's and cloaked with a hood. She was becoming aroused and chose to touch it to appreciate what Peigi had been talking about. Jinti was getting hotter by the minute.

Cinaed's cock was full and firm now. He pumped himself and was not about to move his gaze away from the maids.

"Please show me more tutor love," Jinti all but begged. "I have never even kissed a man!" She shut her eyes briefly as she felt the effects of the mead.

Peigi also was swaying and feeling increased desire. She shifted closer to Jinti and took her face between her hands. "I will show you how it will feel the best. Do you trust me?"

Jinti nodded affirmatively. She wanted to be aware of it all.

Cinaed remained securely against the wall and alternated from a rapid and rhythmic pumping action to an encircling of his thumb and forefinger up and down his cockhead; from tip to frenulum. He craved the completion of their lesson.

Peigi kissed Jinti on the lips. "Keep your lips soft and loose. Follow the lead from your lover, but don't be afraid to kiss back." Peigi and Jinti kissed more fervently now. Practicing the kisses over and over, Peigi kissed Jinti all over her face. "Open your lips and let his tongue enter your mouth like this. Taste the sweetness of his tongue and return with your own favor of sweetness to him . . . mmm".

Cinaed stared in a passionate haze as the maids kissed long and deep, sharing the intimacy of exploring one another's mouth. His cock was rock hard and the dew was beginning to erupt from his mountainous tip. He slowed his pace for a bit as he knew that there were more provocative lessons to come.

Peigi placed her hands on Jinti's breasts and demonstrated to her how a lover would cup them and drag his thumbs over them. Jinti threw her head back and moaned some. Peigi sensed the pleasure that Jinti felt, as she began to buckle beneath it herself. Jinti responded by mimicking Peigi and they moaned and purred together.

Peigi instructed Jinti anew, "Lie with me. Kiss me. Show me how you like to be kissed." Jinti took Peigi's face in her hands and kissed Peigi just right. Jinti was responding beautifully to Peigi's prompts. Such a fast learner Jinti was with pleasure involved.

Hands caressed breasts and Peigi scooted below to show Jinti how the men would suck on her nipples. Jinti had her fingers on Peigi's nipples, squeezing and twisting them, asking Peigi if she could in turn suck her there. Peigi barely nodded, when Jinti's head went to a nipple and nearly bit her tender marble of flesh. "Gently, gently my sweet student. Later the bite of pain will add to the pleasure; let it build". Jinti flattened her tongue and circled around Peigi's nipples. Mmm . . . ohhh . . . yesss . . . nice!

Cinaed experienced this in his own nipples. He gulped the rest of the mead down, and put the goblet on the floor. He used his free hand inside his tunic to stimulate his nipples with his palm. Once erect, Cinaed squeezed and rotated his own nipples, wishing fervently that it was one of the maids doing this to him.

Peigi descended further down the feather bed and situated herself between Jinti's legs. "Open your legs wide. Bend your knees. I am going to give you the gift of ultimate satisfaction tonight." Jinti was very heated by now and willing to do anything that Peigi told her to do. She was much in need of finding the delight of it all.

Peigi's face was so near to Jinti's mound. Peigi's heated breath was there and Jinti instinctively opened her knees wider. Parting Jinti's nether lips, Peigi put her mouth to Jinti's hot bud of reddened flesh and began kissing her softly there. She moved slowly and mildly to allow Jinti to absorb it fully. Jinti moaned and shifted her hips; an indication of heat's beginning onslaught.

Peigi used her tongue flatly to lick the entire pink and shiny bead between Jinti's legs. Moving in a circular motion, she drank in the sweetness of this fresh young woman. When Peigi pointed her tongue and flicked and lashed it at Jinti's clitoris, Jinti nearly fell off the bed.

"Cup your own breasts and find the pleasure that you wish at your nipples right now." Jinti did as suggested and was awash in virginal hot sensation.

"Feel this now, Jinti. There may be a bit of pain as your maidenhead is parted. After that you will experience unique sensations, the first ever for you."

Cinaed was hammering his cock rapidly, attempting to restrain himself as he approached his bursting. He was timing his release with theirs and gauged when to slow and then speed up.

Peigi wet her fingers with moisture from her own mouth, and began caressing Jinti's clit and opening. Jinti's clit responded by swelling out of its hooded cloak. Jinti moaned and raised her hips to meet Peigi's hand.

One finger approached the opening and found a tiny bit of resistance. Peigi pressed on firmly, moving her finger in a circular motion. Jinti moaned and cried out "Yesssss". Two fingers now, pushing to pass the small sheath of skin covering her opening. Oh please yes she wanted this! All the way in now! Jinti gasped!

Peigi worked her fingers in and out of Jinti's opening, whispering words of encouragement for her love to come closer, closer, closer. Jinti's hips moved of their own volition and she rose to meet the rhythm of Peigi's hand. A thumb placed firmly on Jinti's clit took her to that pool of sensation faster now.

"There, feel that . . . feel the burning heat. Let it take you to the pleasure. Don't stop it. Don't fight it. Breathe with it. Yes. Yes. Yes. That's it! You're almost there! Let it happen! Come love, Come!" Peigi brought Jinti over the edge and she cried out as ecstasy swept her up. The spasms rocked Jinti and she cried out. "Onnnnhhhh yes!!!"

Once Jinti's spasms began, Cinaed's cock exploded with his own eruption. He had to keep from crying out himself. His climax was so hard and strong. The cream spurted from him and went everywhere! He bit his lip to keep from growling out in sensation.

Jinti had collapsed back on the bed, eyes closed. She was spent from her first real orgasm. Oh such wonder! She decided that her lovers were to heat her this deliciously or not at all.

Peigi giggled and held Jinti. Jinti giggled right back. "You will be brought to this thrill often. With your voluptuous femininity, oh you will find opportunity after opportunity for yourself."

Cinaed crept silently through the hallways as the two lasses hugged the other and then drifted into a soundless and deep sleep.

This interlude had been so advantageous in distracting him from all that sat heavily upon his mind.

CHAPTER 29

Frustration Mounted

His frustration had only mounted in the passing year. The impasse had not been transformed or broken. It was not like Cinaed to have waited, but he had foolishly done that very thing, as he had hoped for others to have kicked the erected wall standing in the path of the Pictish crown down. He had toyed with what to do and how to do it and that had taken on a life of its own with permutations unending. All were paralyzed in their achievement of that rulership or any of their other special goals that relied on kingship first and then other mighty acts next.

Time was imminent for him to huddle with his most significant counselors and individuals who held wise reason and strategic smarts. So though he loathed going to them, he had no other choice finally. He was caught in his own spider web of possibilities and required the righteous guidance of others to strip that web of its power over him. So he walked singly, having left his entourage behind, to where he discerned Catrione and Eumann were to be found.

He and his mother had had that notable encounter in his royal bedroom so long ago it seemed. She had not presented herself to him alone since. And he had not asked for Eumann's ear in many a season. He was ripe for answers and was even willing to set aside the raw emotions that accompanied his sentiment towards Catrione and Eumann's union in order to acquire what he so desperately sought. The Pictish crown and his joining with that crown that he believed he already owned was his immediate heart's desire. And he was determined to have it . . . now. His pulse quickened at the remotest brush with this thought of successful acquisition for him.

His heart rate was elevated therefore when he located them within their outer chambers. His impulse had been so sudden and strong that he had not considered summoning them to him. And that is why he had gone to them in the instant of this need.

Both his mother and her consort were stunned by his appearance. His mother was the first of the two to catch her wits into a tight fist and exclaim to her son, "m'lord, your presence is so unexpected but so very welcome here. What may we do for you?"

Eumann swiveled in Cinaed's direction, bowed and uttered his "m'lord" as well.

"I am willing to suspend the formalities here as I require advice and answers from either or both of you in a trice.

I am unwilling to postpone my wish to assert my rights to the Pictish crown a moment longer. It is rightfully mine whether by dint of persuasion or force of arms. Do you not agree with me?"

Eumann acceded to his lover as she was his mother and had the privilege of speaking first to her son.

"I am shocked that you, Cinaed, have bided your time this long. I would have guessed that you would have stormed the resistance one way or another already.

I can reply for both Eumann and myself in the affirmative that you have absolute entitlement to that throne simply by your pedigree; a pedigree that I bring to you very strongly as your mother; a princess and Pictish also. What more should be asked of you to produce?"

"They resist me nonetheless!" Cinaed had not confronted his rivals directly in these twelve months that had elapsed so quickly. He simply read them via his powers of insight and knew that their determination to keep the crown from him was vast and deeply entrenched.

"How are you aware of that m'lord?" Eumann queried. He was already privy to the answer but wanted to hear Cinaed reveal it himself to him.

"This is my hour of necessity. So I will request only your focused words here. We are all three of the undead ilk and so we must not mince about or cloak our ideas in games or machinations of any kind. You will be immediately direct with me, clear in your reasoning without guile and, if you are treacherous to me here and now, I will know it! Know that!

In order to begin in a manner that parallels my just expressed sentiments to you, I will divulge openly what has so thoroughly caused me anguish and doubt about the both of you forever it seems.

I loved and cherished my father, Catrione, as you did not. You left his arms so rapidly and I always resented you for that. You felt and knew my resentment. That is why, yes Eumann, my mother and I coupled and never again, I was stunned that we did couple that once. There was, and still is, so much animosity between us, my mother. It had to have been the mead that night because I was ashamed of myself and my cock when I recovered my consciousness also."

Eumann interrupted briefly to calmly say, "Your mother told me of your sexual moment together."

Cinaed went on as if he had not heard Eumann speak whatsoever. "And you, Eumann, I have despised the fact that you took my mother to your bed so swiftly after her marriage to my father. That was a poisonous act and you were only spared because my father either did not know or did not care and I was just a boy. My powers were so limited then. And when my potency became absolute, I needed your wisdom by then and realized that I would slay neither of you.

But I desired to do just that so often!"

Catrione and Eumann were humbled by Cinaed's confession. That they had not performed this feat first made them of obviously lesser morality. Yet they both had their motives and intended broaching them to Cinaed immediately.

Again, Catrione spoke before Eumann. "Your father treated me as chattel. And I understand now that is the way of the Gael male. It is not the way of the Pictish male. They value their women. They even gave us an involvement in the king's selection. Granted, it came with birth and was not earned but it was something; a tidbit for a woman if she was so lucky to have been blessed as queen or princess. I was blessed such.

And your father stole that from me. And it did not concern me that he was ignorant of such. I was not having his ill treatment of me simply because that was all that he understood or was taught.

And Eumann, he was lovely. That he was a tutor and moved from place to place within our neighboring cultures gave him, though he is Gael like you and your father, a sense of the dignity and worth of women. He was of such quality that he absorbed that message and was the only male that

I observed in our city who treated me tenderly and with regard. He loved me. It was obvious.

His capacity for seeing me as a person, not as an item that he owned, not only interested me but allowed me to love him fully."

Cinaed paced the floor as she gave him her explanation of her behavior toward his father. It was disturbing for him as he viewed women with the same chauvinism that his father had. But he was attempting to understand and many of her words penetrated the thick blockade that his culture had instilled in him toward the idea of any egalitarianism toward women. It was most certainly his vampire spirit that had the vast wisdom to permit any understanding of this notion on Cinaed's part.

The vampire within though chuckled as he well knew that he subjugated this wisdom often in the interest of his impetus for blood, violence and quick mistreatment of others.

Eumann interjected as she finished. "Your mother is an incredibly wise woman.

And I love her immensely. And that she loves me in return in spite of her and me being flawed creatures, allows me to love her more so. And I always will.

Her honesty is like a clarion call. She has lineal and physical advantages that she could wield in place of honesty were she that type of individual. But she does not do that. She rather loves to speak clearly and all who hear her know where she stands.

I value your honesty here, Cinaed, equally."

"And I feel identically to you as the two of you speak now. And I consider that, in spite of my full awareness of your thoughts and emotions, to be of inestimable worth. I had decided, obviously, to spare the both of you long ago on the grounds that you Catrione are blood and my mother. And you, Eumann, are her lover and an individual of great capacity.

Strangely, I also felt that if my mother was able to choose you, so was I.

Now do either of you see a means to my acquisition of the Pictish crown?"

Both Catrione and Eumann nodded in the affirmative simultaneously.

CHAPTER 30

Mac Alpin's Treason

"You have to understand that I love my countrymen as I am Pictish born and bred. But Cinaed, you are my son and deserve that throne without reservation.

So for those fundamental reasons, I throw my full weight behind your effort to move to acquire Pictland immediately!"

Eumann half smiled at Catrione as she spoke. He was impatient to get to the plan that he and she had developed for Cinaed. His mother and Eumann had been wary prior about informing him. But now that emotions had been tended to and the air had been cleared, Eumann thrust out what so urgently had to come Cinaed's way.

"Deep in Pictish history, as I learned in the process of teaching lessons to my pupils, men of dreams were assaulted by men acting in opposition to those dreams. So the dreamers, those who chose to expand into territory that was poorly governed by others, did something that was inflammatory and treacherous but done for the better good of all. Or so they thought anyhow.

They invited their enemy to a neutral site with a prior agreement that arms were unwelcome in the encounter between the sides. They gave the idea that this was to be a peaceful meeting their full persuasive abilities. Their adversaries were convinced and the meeting date, time and location were struck.

All met. And of course, it was not meant to be a peaceful encounter. As mead was amply shared, hidden swords and other implements of destruction were summarily presented.

The opposition was obliterated and the threat was wholly eliminated.

These men of dreams took their booty and achieved their expanded kingdom as a place that prospered. In addition, the people served by this action rejoiced.

Cinaed ceased his pacing and nearly shouted, "It is a splendid mode for accomplishing my ends!

Now to the specifics!" He was so obviously eager to settle the details with Catrione and Eumann before departing the vicinity at dawn's first hint. That was hours away but the time would fly as they plotted against the Picts.

During the period of their conspiring, much detail was hammered out.

A principle step included establishing a place for the meeting. And that was worked out without much difficulty. The seat of the kings, as Scone was known, was the ideal location as it had neutrality that other villages and towns did not. The Abbey at Scone had provided many a king, Pictish usually but Dal Riatan occasionally, a lavish site that had been used by one and all.

Moreover, it was within Pictish boundaries, though inhabited by both Picts and Gaels.

Catrione had suggested the idea that a proposal of inducements be sent to each effected party so that they may congregate at this Abbey to resolve the issue of who had the legal justification to guide the Pictish land in leadership.

Eumann pitched in by adding, "The four major parties that have issue with you will have little choice but to respond to your request of assembly. That bidding will actually serve as an informal summons that they must appear. They are encircled by Dal Riata, the unpredictable Viking hoard, and have fewer numbers combined than either we or the Scandinavians have individually. They fear your power and capabilities. It would behoove them to attempt, at least, to honor the proposal and hope that they might appease you in some minor way so that you will leave them to what they believe is their territory.

Throw the bone to the dog so to speak; that you will yield if they can dazzle you with an alternative that truly is of lesser value."

"What might that possibly be, Eumann?"

"A woman whom they sense you might plausibly find to your satisfaction.

That is only one example of many that could be offered to you."

"They think that I am dimwitted. They will feel their comeuppance if they believe that!"

"Stop your emotions instantly.

It does not matter what draws them in, my son. What matters is that they arrive at the Abbey in person and suspect nothing."

"I grasp what you are saying! And it is such wise and deviously good advice!"

So, the trio established the further girding of their audacious plan.

They were to set forth to Scone and the Abbey on the instant.

Once there, they would send their invitations to all who mattered.

They would arrive several days before the gathering and feast following. That would not be suspect as they had initiated the proceedings and therefore would be expected to prepare the Abbey for the session and celebration that the summoned expected on their behalf.

Certain customs were always complied with and this one put Cinaed at an advantage. It gave him cover to establish himself at the Abbey before all others and permit all activity on his part to be thought of as innocent preparation for his worthy visitors. It was to lull the Pictish lords into a false sense of security even while Cinaed had the supremacy and the upper hand over them. Mix that with the fine food and the overwhelming effect of the mead and the atmosphere of high born partying and one had the recipe for deceit, stealth and surprise to overcome their entire foe.

The Columban authority, which owned the Abbey, was not about to be pleased by Cinaed's actions but Cinaed, Catrione and Eumann saw a greater wisdom in what they were about to do. The Church would grasp the wisdom of the Dal Riatan actions soon after the event took place. Of that, all three were certain.

Through the castle's tiny openings to the outdoors, the cluster of vampire's gleaned from the heightened illumination that the minutes remaining for fixing the last established details to their machinations were rapidly vanishing.

The plotters were well satisfied that the design for the trap had been brilliantly conceived, thoroughly established and that all further issues could be and would be dealt with as they occurred.

Cinaed was exploding with positive sentiment and joy. He had to say this to his mother and Eumann before they retired to their especial beds. "I have to give you, my mother, and you, my savvy teacher and esteemed counselor, an array of thanks that even then would not fully display my appreciation for your worthy efforts here. That I have allies of your caliber leaves me no end of confidence in my successful outcome; not only in this endeavor but for endeavors hereinafter."

He then performed extraordinarily. He chastely kissed his mother's cheek and knelt for but an instant before Eumann. In that flash, Eumann was the king and Cinaed the pleased subject. Yet, that Cinaed was able to open and then humble himself cast away most doubt that might have overshadowed his ruling days.

Cinaed left and knew that his mother and Eumann were no longer enemies or evil creatures.

Tears blemished his skin and he wiped them from his eyes as he neared his chambers.

CHAPTER 31

Scone's Embrace

Once the three had consolidated their method by which to seat Cinaed upon his just throne, the small train of Dal Riatans selected to accompany them was established.

He had searched for Aiobheean and her family but had failed abysmally. This would have been the perfect moment to have chosen her to travel with them. He was ready to make amends there. But she and her loved ones were not to be found.

It was early evening and the trek was to take approximately one turn of the moon. They had to be at Scone by sun's reappearance. And they would be.

Here was a reason that he desired discovering Aiobheean's whereabouts; he did not intend to return once gone. He was now devoted to the idea that this relocation was to be a permanent one. In these initial stages, once settled in Scone, he was going to disperse messengers with his claimant's request. And that these requests came from Scone would further reassure the Pictish lords that Cinaed was doing all within his power to accommodate them by this very rearrangement to Scone. They were of the idea, Cinaed was able to see, that this was indubitably only a temporary reestablishment for the sole purpose of the meeting and feasting of them all.

Cinaed, Catrione and Eumann were sorely pleased with how effortlessly they would be able to pacify and dupe these Pictish imbeciles; lords by title, simpletons by behavior.

It was insisted by Cinaed, and agreed to by Catrione and Eumann that the Gaelic coronation stone, the Lia Fail, be transported with them.

It was a large and very weighty slab of grey and red rectangular sandstone that had been brought to Dal Riata from his Gaelic brothers in Ireland several generations ago. It had sat under the throne of Dal Riata for those many years. It had its upper surface scratched deeply from the shifting of the stone over the water between the two kingdoms. It also had a thick iron ring pounded into its right and left sides so that moving the object was made less harsh.

Cinaed was unsure of where precisely he wished to place this stone in Scone as he had never traveled there before. He surmised that the rock was to be repositioned below the throne that already resided at the coronation abbey. By the morrow, he would recognize where for sure.

Eumann leaned to Cinaed. "The stone will, without its mention, just its presence, call attention to the further justification of your instillation as Pictish king. After all, who but a genuine king would have the profound icon of leadership in his possession?"

The King nodded quietly "yes" to Eumann.

Cinaed registered what Eumann had said but his thoughts were truly elsewhere. This Abbey in Scone on Caislean Credi served his purposes so well. It was to house their deadly feast, provide them with the coronation facility and he and his would occupy the Bishop's Palace adjoining the Abbey. The Bishop's Palace was an annex but was vast and magnificent in its own right. And kings past had been content with that as residence. He was not about to change that tradition.

Their only deed now need be their immediate arrival in Scone with the Lia Fail in hand. The Lia Fail had been pried from the throne at Dunadd Hill Fort and was with them now.

He was aware that the Bishop's Palace was empty. That was an accommodation reserved for the one unanimously selected monarch. And it was about to fall into his control.

He let his excitement rise with that knowledge.

The Abbey had previously been informed of their imminent arrival and so it was the moment to move forward and make their way to Scone.

Cinaed, Catrione and Eumann rode their horses on this occasion. They removed all that was necessary in order to avoid a return for anything more. Dunadd Hill Fort had been wonderful but it was well past time to seek a greater horizon.

His mother reminded Cinaed to not bring too much as that would be a first sign arousing suspicion amongst their foe. She had recommended that each individual take what was minimally required for long-lasting change and absolutely no more. Even then, as a last resort, a return for further items to Dunadd was a possibility.

As Cinaed gazed down upon his ranks and kin, he appreciated his mother's advice and believed that they had complied to the highest degree.

He appeared splendid upon his mount, as did Eumann and Catrione. His mother was especially pleasing in her ardor to set forth and in the strong and beautiful aura that she presented.

They went with no emblem or flag of Dal Riata as they ostensibly went in amity and did not prefer to bristle with any hints of aggression.

Their journey lasted exactly as intentioned and Cinaed's small band traversed along the Tay River. As they neared Scone, the land had remained at sea level throughout, their progress slowed some as the ground beneath them grew boggy and saturated with moisture. They were entering the flood plain that encircled the hills of Scone. The waters had receded, as it was the season of the bright and direct sun, but the muddy moss had not quite dried completely beneath their hooves and feet.

Cinaed's followers had no inkling that their leader and those who closely accompanied him were vampires. So he, his mother and Eumann had to be very careful as to their mode of feeding. At Dunadd, they just vanished for brief spans and then reappeared without their absence having been noticed whatsoever. And the three undead were particular, though they preferred other, to kill only animals within the very forest where Cinaed had become a man.

This passage to Scone was more problematic as no one was allowed to sleep this night through. All had to set a pace that was agonizing but had to be endured only this once.

The group had scouts on point to guide the way in the shadows of night. These individuals went on foot and did so only with the aid of torches. They were already familiar with the path that was being taken but conditions were not always the same from one season to the next.

What this triggered was a preoccupation and a fatigue by their numbers except for Cinaed, Catrione and Eumann. Of course, these three relished the night, saw it with brilliant eyes and could have done better than the scouts in bringing everyone to safety in Scone. But they were unable to wield

161

their powers as their true identities would be exposed and their people would have obeyed no longer in their fear and repulsion.

So, no, they remained on their steeds and observed as their entrusted experts fulfilled their roles. How they managed to quench their needs for blood was elementary and successful, fortunately. No one was focused on Cinaed or the other two. Thus, the trio simply rotated their brief departures amongst one another. Cinaed was the first to wing into the dark skies and Catrione and Eumann huddled their horses close to Cinaed's until he returned sated and satisfied. The same was done for Eumann and Catrione.

They risked that the King might be required while Cinaed was absent but they were fortunate to have had no such happening occur. And Catrione and Eumann were not solicited by anyone but Cinaed. So they accomplished what a vampire must and did it without calamity.

At the base of the Abbey's Hill they were greeted by several Columban monks who further escorted them to their only vacant quarters through the Abbey's gates.

Even the monks agreed to put them in the Annex, the Bishop's Palace, as they had Godly information.

CHAPTER 32

Ironic Interlude

The devious epistles had gone out this day to the four. They would be days in their arriving.

Cinaed and his people had been quickly settled in their various quarters as visitors of a short stay would be. The monks were absorbed with spiritual matters and paid little attention to the fact that Cinaed's assemblage was just a mere bit top heavy in the amount of goods that accompanied them to Scone and the Abbey. These monks welcomed all comers to their small Christian sanctuary with open arms.

Cinaed was at the old wood table of one of the superior monks who permanently dwelt in this religious place. They were seated facing one another. The monk grasped a precious book in his hands that had been carefully written and then scribed by the venerable Christian monk and historian, Bede. The author had since passed but the work's subject was that of Columba's evangelical successes. And though it was collected by Bede, many, many quotes of Columba's were peppered throughout.

"I must tend to the prayer session of my fellows now but I crave that you read this and gain a fuller understanding of our Lord and His blessings upon us.

You, of the Dal Riatan territories, in spite of our Gaelic connection and proximity of land, have resisted the total establishment of the Faith more than most.

Once you have perused this volume, the pagan will wash from you as fresh water cleanses the skin."

"Thanks, my kind and generous friend. I will see to its reading in this instant."

The monk stood, handed the tome to Cinaed and then departed with a benign glance Cinaed's way.

Cinaed was left alone with the manuscript and felt the irony in this interlude with what he and his flock intended to do. He was a misbegotten creature about to take the sincerest of script regarding the supposed God above. He believed otherwise about this God with ferocity of undead spirit that clung to his every pore. If he were washed, let the smell of Satan saturate his flesh!

Yet he was curious as well and, in his arrogance, thought himself impervious to spiritual influence. So he delved into the pages without hesitation.

According to Bede, Columba was born in approximately the Year of the Lord five hundred and twenty one. He was of high born Irish status but was carefully groomed for the priesthood by his very fundamentalist parents. From that, he completed his ecclesiastical education and went forth to found Christian monasteries all over his birth country.

In five hundred and sixty three, at the age of forty two, this Columba finished with his Christian duties in his native Ireland and traversed the sea to the British Isles. He journeyed far and fair and convinced the leadership in his new terrain to bestow upon him, for godly purposes of course, the island that became known as Iona.

Lo, the very same land where Cinaed himself had been born.

He read on.

Columba had a strategy that ignited his evangelical fortune throughout the pagan communities. He applied this method to Iona first. He and a Christian compatriot, to begin, pressed the notion of a single god, the mightiest entity of all, upon any who would listen. Once they had enlisted enough converts, these blessed souls built the Columban monastery on that island from logs and reeds. With its completion, Columba left twelve to tend to the greater conversion of those neighbors nearby his core church.

At the same time, Columba departed for the wild, barbaric and unconverted regions. Dal Riata was ignored as Columba made the mistaken assumption that his own Gaelic brethren were already of Christian sympathy. So he trekked to the northeast into Pictland, sometimes called Caledonia, to the southeast into Northumbria and, finally, back to what was initially the southwest region of Strathclyde.

He laid special emphasis on converting the Pictish as they seemed the least likely to be persuaded. That was the kind of man that Columba was.

Then, upon entry into these untamed regions, he sought out the most influential individual in residence there. That was, inevitably, the king. If Columba's presence was refused by that monarch, he proceeded with the next royal in line. He was never deterred and ultimately converted a vast number to Christianity.

As well, his original monastery emphasized ecclesiastical education over basic asceticism and spiritual retreat. His church in Iona was not meant for solitude and isolation, certainly not. It was launched for the vital purpose of learning the godly word and then planting that word in the heart of their neighbor's chests.

The method therefore, was to take a vibrating and radiant fundamental belief, build a hut or dwelling or whatever was manageable as a monastery, educate converts to carry on the spiritual work just absorbed, have Columba and a few of his best and most fervent then go out to expanded sections and locate the most influential person there. After that, simply persuade that significant target to believe as Columba believed and ascribe to this pattern of expansion redundantly and infinitely.

That was what Columba, were he alive as Cinaed scanned the pages, would have told one and all was the manner and mode to fruitfully entice disbelievers into the sweet embrace of the one true God.

Cinaed silently smirked at the naïve sentiments that jumped from the page to his eyes.

If there had been a benign and benevolent god, Cinaed and his kind, vampires of the harsh and ugly night, would never have been created. How could a loving god do that to his people!? Or, for that matter, to allow Cinaed's own breed to be so vile.

He hissed at the idea of a beneficent god who protected his inventions.

Then, for an instant only, a thought blew through Cinaed's brain. What if this god had a plan, a slow moving but righteous plan? Then the thought vanished as quickly as it had arrived.

He saw the advantages of his entourage residing in the House of the Lord though. Who would guess that a bloody maneuver was to take place here in this very spiritual temple? No one would dream that the apostate was sitting in the very place of the cross.

The ancient idea of the Church itself holding sway over and beating back the vampire was utter nonsense. It was the equivalent belief that a vampire had to be invited in to come in. A vampire was able to go wherever there was human wickedness. And since each and every human had a portion of that within them, the undead went everywhere.

To the deluded human mind, this dwelling was meant as a safe zone and a spiritual sanctuary, was it not?

It was not. Cinaed discerned the reality!

He was godless and was not giving up his design to slaughter the Picts. And it would occur in this very house!

He snapped the good book closed!

CHAPTER 33

Seen and Unseen

Eumann stepped lively and nearly stumbled in his rush to reach Cinaed. He waded through the King's regal crowd and interrupted Cinaed mid-sentence. Cinaed's trusted henchman, also designated enforcer of Cinaed's rules through all daylight hours, glared at Eumann but Cinaed whipped his head Eumann's way and then demanded, "Everyone, leave me at once!"

Yes, Eumann, speak to me."

Eumann forgot the courtesies to his King in his excitement to bring Cinaed news of what he had just observed while in the monk's hallways and quarters.

"Cinaed, you must accompany me this instant. You will not believe your eyes upon this looking. Do not use your powers. Let this be a joyous surprise!

It must also be an indication, a foreshadowing, of the positive outcome of our tactics for the Picts. This can be nothing but a sign of wonderful tidings to come!

And do not bother to dress in kingly raiment. We must hurry. You are fine as you are."

The two almost collided with one another as they bolted out the King's door simultaneously. Cinaed had to yield a bit to his now friend and counselor as Eumann knew their precise destination on this occasion.

Moments later, Cinaed had his hand well over his gasping mouth as he gazed upon a view that he had longed for oh these many years.

Yes, Aiobheean sat with what must have been their son at the very table with the very monk that Cinaed had done the evening prior.

Dusk had just alighted and cast its shadow over the countryside outdoors.

So why were they here and engaged in concentrated, demonstrative conversation with this monk at this hour?

Eumann quietly exited the area as his duty to Cinaed had been fulfilled.

As if in a dream, Cinaed permitted his eyes to linger where there was so much to cherish in the vision of his eternal love, Aiobheean. Even from her backside and seated, she stunned him and his desire for her shot above and beyond anything felt or sensed by him before.

Her long, thick and heavily braided hair fell over the chairs supports and almost to its legs as well. Another inch or so and the strands would have brushed the floor. Those multitudinous strands were of the strawberry blond color contained within his memory but it also was naturally streaked with more blond than in her youth. He was able to visualize her face somewhat as she turned slightly every time that she spoke in what was, on this occasion at least, a very pronounced and animated style. Because of this, her cheeks flashed in his direction repeatedly. From this, he noted that her skin was still porcelain-like, rosy but with a lesser flush of pink tint to the supple flesh there. Her girlish freckles seemed to have disappeared as her years advanced too.

He imagined that her eyes remained the gorgeous aquamarine blue with their hints of green and gold.

But why surmise when he could realize her entirety!?

So, at this point, he loosed the restraints of his undead power in order to espy her full luster within his mind. He considered her as if she stood closely in front of him, nude, and did not move nary a muscle. What he perceived was a gleam beyond beauty. She had captivated him once as a just turned man and that now morphed into a further delight and a wanting that flew past anything he thought he was capable of experiencing for anyone or anything.

The person that he examined posing at his behest on his mind's screen was breathtaking. She had a tiny upturned, come hither yet wise smile upon her. Those lips were stained the magnetic raspberry that she had then and now.

His visualization was beyond his control and his inner attention dropped from her lush and entrancing lips to an even larger bust than she had had in their original entwining.

He had to rework the position of his cock as it was surging in its throb that required her grasp. He wore only a thin cloak and a light set of ankle length trews. His cock was distinctly noticeable when soft but was massive here and he had to angle it somewhat to the side to avoid having it simply expand past the upper band of his clothing there. Dew was cascading from his very plump and pulsing plum-like tip. The hard redness of it expressed everything regarding his wish for her.

At other times, he would have been embarrassed and ashamed at the strength and show of his need. But now, other than to maneuver his thick and lengthy column in those trews, his attention was riveted upon her overarching figure in his mind and the reality of her in her chair.

Her force over him was so commanding that Constantine did not draw his eyes yet.

That bigger bosom entranced him no end as he remained rooted to the floor. His faculty for comprehending her totality informed him of that which fascinated and paralyzed him now. Her chest had been enormous on such a lean frame in her adolescence. How her frame had handled her mounds earlier had been a conundrum almost. In this instant though, her sloping curves were even more pendulous than they had been. There was an obvious elongation of much thicker and quite pronounced nipples in addition.

She had been suckled often by child, at the least, in his long absence.

His palms and fingers itched to make contact with her heaviness there. His fingers and mouth craved touch with her intensively.

The lean frame was thin yet. Her age had worked their years on her in such subtle manner. Her barely built upon still slender lines gave her form greater femininity and a lithe appeal that she had not had so much of previously. She had been composed of firmer angles then where she was rounded and filled further now. Her belly was gently pronounced with a miniscule layering of pliant flesh added to her thighs and buttocks. Her legs persisted in their muscled and toned manner.

His internal images and actual sight meshed and flowed together in a swift and efficient spin that was compelling.

In this contemplation of his, she had not left her chair nor even become aware of his presence.

His son had no idea of who his father was.

Suddenly, his rapture was broken. Aiobheean and Constantine pushed from their chairs and stood in order to depart.

Cinaed knew that it was a friendly leave taking. The monk kissed the back of her outstretched hand and patted Constantine on his cheek.

In concern, Cinaed's henchman appeared and stopped several paces behind his King.

Cinaed was utterly confidant that his construction of Aiobheean, seen and unseen parts, was absolutely precise and rigorously exact.

As she placed her arm around her son's back and began to guide him to the Abbey's exit, she looked peripherally.

Cinaed held his stance momentarily as her forward motion ceased entirely.

He was well aware that she was in disbelief and shock. The fleet collapse of her beautiful face would have registered on a blind man.

Cinaed was in no manner remotely blind. And cognizant that he had been accurate in every detail.

CHAPTER 34

Constantine My Son

She beat upon his chest and wept and sobbed copiously all the while panting out the vilest names she was capable of conjuring up for Cinaed. She was purging herself of eleven years of pent up rage at his youthful abandonment of her and their child.

Constantine had attempted to restrain her as she wrathfully ran at the standing chiseled mountain of a man. Her son had been no match for the wild fury's energy that his mother displayed in abundance. She was a hurricane of pain released for all to see.

Cinaed let her thrash him as he had sworn to himself that were he and his love ever to meet again, she had every right to hammer him into dust and then sweep that dust from her sight.

He had been so ashamed of his boyish reaction when she had told him of her pregnancy. But he had not had the nerve or courage to locate her and apologize profusely. When his bravery and love had finally found their tipping point within him, just before this sojourn, he had failed resoundingly in this. Her more aged parents were not even at the wheelhouse when it had been checked.

In his haste to arrive in Scone and in his dense sadness at what he deemed a profound and eternal loss, he had forgotten to achieve his ends via his seer seeing ability. But now he knew the reason for her absence. She lived no longer in Dal Riata but had established herself, Constantine and her parents in Scone. He suspected that her grief had been the driving force behind the change.

He chose to hear her probably very emotionally charged explanation later and did not resort to his vision in these hours.

What he did realize for sure was that she would expose her feelings of that period to him soonest; but not until she calmed, of course.

Now he had to permit her to flail and bang her fists against him until her current seemingly bottomless pit of hostility towards him had abated. He was stirred in the deepest and saddest of manner for her travail in the period of their separation. There was to be no further parting between them. To the degree that he was in control of that, henceforth, it was always to be.

Finally, he held her and brushed swollen and heartfelt apologies, then frequent requests for forgiveness into her hair, at her ears, to her neck, upon her eyelashes; anywhere that she allowed him his whispered entreaties to her. He lifted his grief stricken eyes to Constantine often enough as well.

Eventually, she began to subside and mellow. Cinaed and Constantine assisted her back to the chair she had warmed earlier. She needed it but for a moment and then stood winded and shaking as she faced Cinaed again and then sought his outstretched arms.

Constantine peered at Cinaed and silently queried him.

"Yes, my son, I am your father. And I am so sorry!"

The monks and Cinaed's henchman all lowered their eyes as if they had just been chastised. But it was not that whatsoever. They were wise enough to not interfere where none of them were required or desired. Cinaed, Aiobheean and Constantine were given their own path to take through this tangle. The monks receded out of view so gracefully and quietly that their presence was as if it had never been.

The henchman moved to the opposite side of the table from Cinaed and his family momentarily, focused across to the trio as he leaned in to study the scene more closely but, of a sudden, decided his aid was unnecessary. He too departed as of a ghost decomposing into mist and fog.

Cinaed embraced his son to him and Constantine did not resist. With passing time and a continued embrace, Constantine actually began to yield into his father's chest where he laid his temple against his mother's temple; she was already there as her head had sunk into his torso long ago. His huge arms spanned them both and he had finally come home.

Aiobheean slowly reached her arms around Cinaed's waist and besides resting her face upon him, laid her ample chest into him. Aiobheean and Constantine moved with no intent whatsoever except to feel his skin a first time for him and once again for his mother.

He used his seer capacities again in this second and discerned how profoundly she missed him; she had never taken another lover to her chambers though many had tried and failed. Cinaed had mingled with his mother and was to broach this subject with Aiobheean at a more appropriate moment; a moment where, he was sure, she would understand. She would feel for him as he planned on persuading her that it had been a harsh mistake provoked by the inebriating influence of the mead. Later on that though; much later.

Constantine carried a linen handkerchief with him and wiped his mother's eyes gently. She had released her clutch of Cinaed and he of her and they stepped back a pace to gaze at the other in a soft earnestness now that the gale had swept by. She tenderly stroked Cinaed's cheek and then scrutinized her son briefly. She steadied herself, took in a breath and introduced the two.

"Constantine, this is Cinaed, your finally father.

"Cinaed, this is Constantine, your always son."

The man and his offspring studied the other dispassionately for but an instant.

Aiobheean was frozen in anticipation and expectation.

Cinaed was pitched then into a pool of emotion as the swirl of words labored to fly from his lips. All that breached his lips though was, "Oh Constantine, my son, my son!"

The son and the father were much similar although Constantine was not yet near as massive as his father.

He had his mother's paleness and blond hair which was plaited to the side in the custom of the day. He had his mother's thoroughly blue and guileless eyes. His lips, though manly, were full as well. She had given him that in addition.

There was so much besides succor that she had bestowed upon Constantine.

So what was there remaining for Cinaed to share with him?

Genes he had already provided.

But there was so much more for him to donate to his son here on. He would provide Constantine with his protection, his wisdom, his care, his wealth, his kingship eventually and the all-encompassing promise that he was never to leave their sides again.

And then he kissed Constantine on the brow.

Constantine kneeled before his father as it was known far and wide who Cinaed was.

CHAPTER 35

Choker's Revelation

A dissimilar monk strode out to Cinaed, Aiobheean and Constantine and took Constantine's shoulder in his tight grasp.

"Your interest is in becoming, like me, a servant of the Faith and of this Abbey. It is quite a mature ambition for one who is only eleven. I applaud your wisdom.

Let me be your guide for some hours tonight and allow me to instruct you in the manners of this Church. You will be most pleased to view our service from the inner sanctum."

As Constantine was led, mesmerized and enthusiastic, off to hallways ahead, the monk turned his head quickly to Cinaed and Aiobheean. It was then that he, surprisingly, gave the pair a wink.

"I will love him. That sense surrounds me already.

And I have always loved you Aiobheean."

She shushed him with her forefinger to his lips.

"As I love you my darling Cinaed.

And Constantine has a great heart. He will recognize your quality and allow his anger to vanish; as I have done in a trice.

So that you understand, Constantine desperately wishes to carry out the work of this Christian Faith. You could tell that, I know, but I had to be certain of your knowledge there; so that is why these words to you.

Use that tact with him and you will find not only kin in him but an ally you can forever count on."

Cinaed held her hand tightly as they comfortably strolled to his boudoir.

His people were amazed that their King was not only with a woman romantically but was obviously in thrall to her; and she to him.

Cinaed waved all away as they entered his chambers. And, as usual and without hesitation, they fled elsewhere.

"My love, I have a single edgy question to ask you. You no longer wear my choker round about your neck? I observed it on the aid that shadows you always.

Am I to think you have disregarded my wholehearted gift to you? It was the sincerest token of my love for you. Did my gesture mean nothing?"

As Aiobheean wound up in intensity over this subject, Cinaed was aghast at the direction her questions were taking and had to stop her concern before it damaged the repair that had just now occurred.

"I sometimes do not wear it but do treasure it so that I do not want it stolen! So, when I periodically chose to leave my neck bare, and as he is one of my most trusted advisors, I approve him placing it around his own neck."

"I crave laying it upon you soon. Bring him here once we have dallied please."

What was Cinaed to do? He had to comply. But the silver of the choker would sear his throat as it did all vampires and he had not worn it since the bloody battles of eight thirty four.

He would find a way to side step her request though. Building their rapport was all that concerned him presently.

"I will have him place it in your hands after we have tarried here and then you may do exactly as you hanker to do."

He had stalled her temporarily and hoped that their elevating sense for one another would act as amnesia upon her and she would forget her request entirely.

Instead of the routine tunic, Aiobheean wore a tunic that was somewhat contrary to a visit to an abbey, but oh well, and that tunic had a delicate and nearly sheer white linen bodice. All that was hidden quite effectively by the heavy grey woolen and hooded cloak that she had thrown over the tunic to endure the cold chill of the ever darkening eve.

In chambers, though, the hearth was lit with the blistering flame and it removed the chill that tended to dwell in the rooms of the Abbey. It was hot and Aiobheean's inclination was to peel her cloak off. She was not quick enough as Cinaed came to her in his nearly nonexistent hoodless cloak and leg length trews. He locked his gaze with hers and then they simultaneously dropped their eyes to his smooth and carefully focused motion that parted her cloak from her chest.

The linen strained in its effort to maintain the position of her mounding curves. Her thick, long and gloriously pointed nipples stirred his loins into regaining the hard and full erection he had lost while tending to Aiobheean's anger's needs.

This episode, he did not have to shift his thriving erection. He let his crimson knob grow past the upper band of his trews. His cock covered his naval and was wide and thick. The trews performed as a mild tourniquet would and he throbbed incredibly. His faint bluish side vein pulsed and his cock seeped dew and jerked at irregular intervals in his anticipation.

She groaned at his first delicate stroke of both reaching, yearning nipples of hers. Her aureoles had almost disappeared in their puckered constriction and pushed her nipples even more forward in that process. At this contact of his, she swooned into his arms and he lifted her easily and so tenderly draped her longwise on his luxurious bed.

He suckled her nipples through her material and they were so elongated and large around, it was as if he tongued the distal portion of a woman's thumb. The fields of flesh that these nipples of hers were centered upon were widespread and high raised.

She moaned when he lifted his head from her nipples and kneaded her breasts with fingers palsied in their excitement upon her.

He refrained no longer. He sat her upright; just enough to lift her tunic from her body. Her breasts cascaded heavily towards him. They were so ample that he had to knee walk backwards slightly in order to cup them and stroke them with his fingers.

She untied his trews then and fully released his column. He removed his trews and flung his cloak to wherever. They were both completely stripped and nude now.

She tugged at his cock and kissed it, pumped it, sucked it wildly in her yearning need for him. He was equally frantic for her, laid her back down, and rotated so that she was melded to his pulsing member and he was pumping her vault with his big and long fingers. He fed on her gleaming crimson pebble there avidly. Her taste was exquisite and she trembled and whimpered more loudly as he continued his attention to her jewel.

He anticipated coming in her mouth but truly had to have his prod gloved within her vault. So he parted from her nether lips and reversed his stance once more. He straddled her and bent to her exposed nipples as she spread her legs wide for him. He lifted her ankles to his shoulders too so that her openness was the greatest possible and invited his soon to be thrusts in without a doubt.

She was drenched in her passion's wetness but he was so large that she guided him carefully deep inside her anyhow.

She arched toward him involuntarily when he was planted within her. He held and she writhed on his pole. The build for this had been years in the coming.

Aiobheean panted and gasped as he remained still and had her pinned to the bed.

Then he was no longer in control of himself. He drove in and out of her at a speed that blurred. He continued to bend and sup at her nipples while pounding at her nether flesh. Their pelvis's collided over and over and the vibration of that was intense for Aiobheean. She felt it throughout her swollen clit.

She had her fingers tangled in his hair at his nape and pushed his head into her breast.

Her panting escalated. He growled and savored the pleasurable pain that he knew she was experiencing as he unleashed himself upon and within her.

"Please my love, harder, faster, deeper. Drive it through me if you must! Yes! Please, oh please!"

She clutched him suddenly, her head reared and her hips sprang upward; she cried and moaned and shook as her waves, her thunderous release, drew the same monster sensation out of him. His load into her, her spasms for him were furious and splendid.

He had loosed a huge amount of pearly come into her. She loved that filled and completed feeling from him.

He lay beside her with his head balanced in his palm. He dreamily relived the coupling just finished in his mind.

"Bring him, Cinaed. I will see it upon you now."

Cinaed was as if syrupy and unable to resist her gentle command. He could stall no more.

He called for his henchman as they covered themselves.

"Place it in her hand."

The henchman did.

"Go now."

And he did.

Cinaed stayed immobile, poised for the heat and pain of it.

Aiobheean had no idea of what was about to transpire. She encircled it side to side at his throat. His skin charred instantly and she flung it from him!

"Oh my love, I am so incredibly sorry!"

"I will heal.

And I will reveal what you have exposed in the silver's harsh effect on me.

I am vampire. And that saved my life while in past crisis. It was a blessing for me."

She kissed him then where he had been burned and wept that she cared not.

CHAPTER 36

Parchment Forgotten

Cinaed had called for this gathering of Aiobheean's participation; he felt her analysis was necessary in sorting through and fine tuning the strategy for Pictish massacre.

Eumann had appeared with Catrione and the single hastily scribed copy of their plans for the righteous deed.

The lords had received their invitations and all had assented. What other choice did they really have? And it was to take them several days to present themselves before Cinaed. So Cinaed had two nights for preparation of the feast's room at the most. This then was to be the only meeting of these singular minds over this particular matter ever.

It was just the four of them with the henchman guarding the entryway. Cinaed introduced his found love to Eumann and Catrione as they had never actually met face to face. The pleasantries were very informal and exchanged quickly as Eumann and Catrione had a full sense of Cinaed's involvement with and regard for Aiobheean already. Additionally, time was short and of the essence.

Eumann got to the heart of the matter abruptly therefore. He pulled the precious parchment from between his tunic and cloak. It was folded in an unimpressive rectangle but was of excruciating importance nonetheless and should have been enclosed somehow.

Eumann spieled these words to begin. "Aiobheean, we believe this to be a very satisfactory approach to seeing Cinaed to the Pictish throne. He has announced his claim and too many years have passed in the meantime. The moment is ripe for action and the taking of his throne." Catrione vigorously nodded in the affirmative. Cinaed did nothing except to closely follow Aiobheean's reactions and responses. He too, as with his mother and her lover, favored the present method devised but waited while Aiobheean was apprised of each and every detail that was pertinent.

Catrione reminded Aiobheean that Catrione was a Pictish princess and that was all that was truly required for Cinaed's succession. Then she deferred to Eumann as he explained the multitudinous other items that solidified Cinaed's stake here.

To Aiobheean, she was fervently convinced here and now of her love's entitlement to the lands that surrounded Scone; and, of course, the established crown in his possession already.

"So the Pictish lords argue your claim? To this day? How can they? Yours is the obvious and weightiest of all the applications for that royal seat!"

Cinaed did speak then. "They know me not and resist all that I claim and offer once crowned in Pictland. This will be the sole opportunity to have met with them.

They know only fable, rumor and ill reports of me. They seem committed to the proposition that their rule would be superior to mine, especially Drust IX.

And they doubt that I am my mother's son.

But as Catrione and I stand together before them, well then, they will see that I am my mother's son.

And they will also feel our united wrath as well!"

"Then show me in detail your scheme for their killing," Aiobheean requested.

Eumann pointed her, line by line, step by step, through their strategy.

The requests had been sent he said. Those requests had been responded to and that most likely meant that the lords anticipated presence was to be within two turnings of the moon.

Further, the lords were to come unarmed as they were informed that Cinaed was equally so. And, of course, this was not to be as Cinaed was to be armed aplenty. The five, the lords and Cinaed with their seconds, were to discuss entitlements civilly and then, regardless of any forthcoming solution, there was to be a feast and celebration of the many so that one and the other might become more familiar.

Mead was to flow too.

In the prior forty eight hours preceding the exultant joining of Picts and Gaels, a rush to redesigning the banquet hall was to ensue. Pits were to be dug underneath the designated benches for the Picts, those earthen hollows filled with long blades, hilts firmly buried in the ground with sharp blades pointing skyward. There were to be rows and rows of the lethal weapons side by side. Some kind of wood platform was to cover these pits. Hinges and bolts were to permit the Gaels, upon Cinaed's signal, to pull the several pins, loose the bolts, work the hinges and have the camouflaged trap doors fall down and away perfectly. The Picts, inevitably, by their very mass, were to plunge to the swords below and sent instantly to their just reward in the afterlife.

The parchment had been written out with sketches of pit location, number of swords to be used, trap door setups and how they were to be best disguised.

Aiobheean was awestruck. Cinaed observed this to be so. What he did not grasp and was shocked by momentarily thereafter was that Aiobheean was struck, not by the quality of the plan or the viciousness of it but, ultimately, by the absurdity of it.

"You cannot do this my love! It will be, without doubt, impossible to accomplish successfully!

You have forty eight hours only to dig the pits, plant the swords and build the trapdoors. You then have to do all this quietly so that the monks will not know of the desecration of their Abbey that you perform. After, you have to remove the dirt from the site without being noticed by spies or other significant folk. In addition, the disguised trap doors have to be done seamlessly so that they will not be discovered. And then you have to manage to get at least eight very inebriated, willful and powerful men to sit just so.

And there is the factor as well that you can never be certain that these rebellious lords will come unarmed as requested and not without their own scheme!"

It cannot be done Cinaed. Please believe me!"

"I am the King. It can be done!

Though I have had my doubts on occasion."

Eumann and Catrione were stunned and hushed. They both were cognizant that any further discussion was to be exclusively between Cinaed and Aiobheean.

"You are the King and my king as well. But you are not well advised to do this.

My apologies to Catrione and Eumann but significant flaws have been overlooked. It will only result in your disaster, demise and ridicule amongst the Pictish populace."

"What are your proposals then my lovely and wise partner?"

"Oh my god Cinaed, don't you see? Do you not understand? Persuade them with your words, your entitlement, your mother's Pictish strength, your magnetism, your wise plans for their future as their king, your magnanimity and most of all, your resoundingly sweet goodness.

You are so capable my wondrous love of this route to your positive achievement and I beg of you to follow that path!"

Cinaed sighed and went to his Aiobheean. He lifted her trembling chin tenderly and kissed her deeply.

She was his savior and his salvation.

Eumann and Catrione had no further say in the matter.

The parchment was tucked out of sight behind the nearest book flap. It was then forgotten and only to be discovered centuries later.

CHAPTER 37

Readily Agreed

The brothers Mac Ferat, that being Brude, Kynat and Drust IX with Bruide Mac Fotel, came collectively to the royal city of Scone. The wind dusted the forelocks and manes of the nearly dozen mounts with riders who had reined to a stop as they drew to Scone's outskirts. It was cautionary as they chose to scout out the area briefly before they rode in en masse.

None had been stupid enough or brazen enough to have encountered Scone and Cinaed on their own. They were often harsh, quarrelsome, hot tempered at the slightest insult or perceived grievance, inclined to rash and violent acts but they were not gullible or blind to the ways of their many enemies. The Gaels and Danes, the Angles and Saxons, the Strathclydes and Northumbrians had seasoned these Picts. They ventured forth in defensiveness, especially when invited. They were alert and disciplined so as not to be anyone's victim.

They had just separated from their own significant number of soldiers encamped beyond the encircling tree line. Vision was scant this eventide and after their several scouts led on, the lords trotted forward, silent and vigilant as could be.

A monk, Cinaed, Eumann and Cinaed's henchman were at the Abbey's entry when the Picts rode up to the monastery's outer perimeter. The monk functioned as gracious intermediary between the two rival groups. The tension was palpable but the servant of God did his best.

Cinaed nodded to each and every Pict. All four of these tattooed lords eyed Cinaed warily. This was not a meeting of the hale and hearty sort. Suspicion abounded and their doubts were reflected in their behavior.

Drust IX Mac Ferat had dismounted first and appeared to Cinaed to set the pace and tone for the others. This baffled Cinaed somewhat as Drust, stout and able performing, had not the physique that the others had. Though there was not a Pict of the now dismounting individuals who had the monumental frame to match Cinaed, they all were big, burly and towering men.

Cinaed and Drust clasped forearms and executed a subtle and almost too quick to be noticed tug of war. Men were always testing one another. In this case, neither prevailed nor had they intended to.

The monk indicated that the Gaels and Picts follow him into the mouth of the Abbey. The monk instilled trust as the Church was ostensibly neutral. So the wordless stomp of warriors moved fluidly to a hall made ready for the communion of the two divided clusters.

Drust began in imperious and rough manner. "What have you to present to us that should make us regard you as anything but a false and inferior claimant.

There is nothing new for you to assail us with.

But begin and try. It will be fleeting at best and we will refuse as has been our custom over time."

The various monks attended to the participants and supplied mead to the adversarial assembly as a matter of courtesy and decency. It was presumed that the Pictish had ridden long and ridden hard. Their thirst had now to be quenched.

Cinaed whispered to his henchman who instantly departed to fetch Catrione. She was a critical piece in Cinaed's declaration and presentation in this hour. "I await my mother's presence. I wished her warmth and so did not have her waiting and chilled outside. My man goes to get her immediately as you have now arrived and your needs have been tended to."

The small Pictish hoard mutely quaffed their refreshments while Cinaed and Eumann stood their ground surrounded by the supremely hostile energy emanating from the almost bristling lords.

Catrione was escorted into the hall by Cinaed's henchman. A female's attendance here, and a Pictish female at that, gentled the room right away. Her beauty left the lords in a somewhat awed and slightly contrite stance in addition. How were they to take the measure of this Pictish woman? The emotional imbalance that she caused confused and stirred them simultaneously and weakened their initial bravado without a doubt.

Cinaed and Catrione positioned themselves jointly and jointly fronted their foe. The irony and strangeness of the Pictish princess confronting her blood brethren with a decidedly unfriendly mien and intent disconcerted Drust and his allies to the utmost.

"I am Pictish and this is my son, Cinaed. I attest to that and for any of you to doubt that is the equivalent of heresy. I spawn kings of Pictland! As my son with Alpin, he deserves that!

Observe us very closely. There are resemblances that are absolute and indisputable."

The lords peered at the mother and son standing before them and recognized physical traits whose similarity were not to be denied.

"Regardless, my word is not one that you may trifle with or challenge. My lineage is without question. Cinaed as Pict is without question. Cinaed as the King of the Picts should be without question as well!"

Cinaed interjected then and enumerated those sound rationales of kith, kin, clan and possession of the Lia Fail that had been previously expressed by him to them in writing repeatedly.

Drust, Brude, Kynat and Bruide listened to every word that poured from Cinaed's mouth. And they had heard these selfsame arguments in years gone by.

Yet there was something about viewing Catrione in person that was wielding an impact that had not weighed on them when claims were flung at them from a distance. They discerned that they were softening and yielding; but not because of Cinaed. Catrione was having a profound and pronounced effect on all of them.

Admittedly, Cinaed's bloodline was rather convincing. Their stubbornness as an entitlement was as poor a reason as existed. And how much longer could they ignore him without going to war with Dal Riata? And their warriors were considerably taxed due to the conflicts they had been involved in in eight hundred and thirty nine. War with Cinaed was most likely a failed cause for them therefore. Drust, the clearest thinking of the four, was the individual who was maximally struck by the multiple implications of what consequences resistance to Cinaed was apt to bring.

Cinaed continued in spite of using his powers to be privy to Drust's cogitations in particular. Cinaed understood that his obligation to persuade the Picts had already been accomplished. Aiobheean had been correct and words, not violence, were carrying the day; or night as the case was. He continued because he felt compelled to detail his ideas for Pictland under his rule. His urgency to be magnanimous and downright decent was beyond his control at the moment. So he laid out the code that his kingdom, Alba, Pict and Gael alike, was to experience.

"I will initiate laws that will protect the weak and the less fortunate. Theft will be accompanied by hanging and murder will beget beheading of the perpetrator. Blasphemers shall have their tongues removed. Neighbors who lie about their fellow neighbors shall be shunned and disarmed. We will enact laws that give a number of men the power to determine punishments in individual crimes that I have not even yet contemplated. I will see that farmers and serfs, the Church and its clergy will be treated fairly.

I will lead beneficially. I will consider Gael and Pict alike as equals."

Catrione joyously intoned, "That is my son whom you listen to! He must be your king and you must see to that! I will have nothing other!"

Drust and his men were speechless.

After seeking eye contact with his two brothers and Bruide, he capitulated.

"Cinaed, you are our king. We readily agree to that fact!

To the coronation!" They hoisted their goblets Cinaed's direction together.

The next eve, the feast that might have been violent was not.

Cinaed, while eating and drinking abounded, leveled his loving gaze at Aiobheean.

CHAPTER 38

Lia Fail

In eight hundred forty two, the rebellious Wrad was defeated by Cinaed.

In eight hundred forty three, once the foundation for agreement was formed for his kingship over Pictland, Cinaed had his fatal stone, the Lia Fail, inscribed thus, "If fates go right, where'er this stone is found . . . . the united peoples shall monarchs of that realm be crowned."

He had the one hundred and fifty three kilogram sandstone slid onto newly created solid ledges of wood underneath the throne itself. The throne was three sided, loomed high and had carved wood feet in the shape of lions.

The stone meant so much to Cinaed. It was the signifier of rulership and also by dint of its consistent use at coronations for generations connected the line of his people together through the millennia.

He had to chuckle in spite of his seriousness regarding the stone as he was reminded of the superstitious notion that, if a rightful claimant sat upon the throne above the stone, the stone was to groan. Silence from the stone boded a pretender for sure.

What unmitigated nonsense Cinaed pondered.

He played out the details of his coronation in his mind's eye. It was not a grandiose coronation as had been the performance at Dunadd Hill Fort. It was indoors in the Abbey's throne room. The crowds were to await both the ceremony and the feast at the Abbey's perimeter only.

Much of the plans simply applied themselves to the routines of tradition. That left much specific handiwork to be done even so. This labor was not to fall on him though. He was principally to be fitted for his lush kingly attire and answer those several questions regarding his preferences. All else was already established and marked out.

He had made basically only one major request. He had insisted upon the absence of the Druid at his side. His pagan beliefs had been shifting greatly since his and Aiobheean's revival. He wished to influence Constantine positively and so was to emphasize the Christian sway in his ceremony.

This meant that, as he sat ensconced in his royal chair and was in process of being crowned, to his right elbow, in this order of nearest to furthest, was to stand the Columban priest, then Eumann and thirdly his henchman. To his left elbow, again in the same orderly fashion as his right, was to stand another Columban priest, then his gorgeous queen, Aiobheean, and lastly his lustrous mother.

Aiobheean was positioned second as she and Cinaed had performed their blissful required nuptials an evening ago. Her father had gladly signed documents giving his daughter over to Cinaed for a bride price that was adequate to her value. Cinaed cherished and loved her so. He almost would have paid her father the new kingdom he had just acquired for her. Her father asked for much less and the documents had been signed. The priest present had bound them in a covenant before the one God, the couple had held hands and whispered their deeply felt "I do's" to one another. Then parents and priest had departed and left the couple to consecrate their love in ecstatic embrace.

When his crown was so graciously placed upon his bare head this time it was to be a crown of simple gold. For effect, he would not wear his warrior's helmet beneath the golden circle situated regally at his occiput. He had shown his prowess many a time over. The populace was aware of his skill and bravery there. He desired that they look upon his proudly plaited hair with gleaming gold above and see that emblem only. He was their king with the crowning and his warrior aspect was only a fraction of how he was to lead. They had to be shown his totality only during this ceremony.

Then there was the feast. Those who were undead were to rotate individually to the out of doors and find their crimson sustenance. Done one at a time, their absence would not register with any of the humans here. So the vampires were consigned to surveillance of the unfolding scene only and did not partake of the refreshments.

The feast was to be a thing of beauty and of great and joyous pleasure. Throughout that celebration, Aiobheean was to hang close by him. He would have it no other way and he believed that she felt like minded. And, if she did not, he would command her. This brought an inner guffaw as he was never intending on commanding her.

She must do his bidding out of her love for him; never as subject or vassal.

How would the feast unfold?

He contemplated the entertainment first. The music was to consist of horns, the trumpa, the delicate bone flute and, of course, a drum beat to pound out a sensual rhythm and flow for the party at hand. To layer greater sensuality upon the musical influences of the repast, there was to be a myriad of female dancers with scant attire, aesthetic art of the skin flashing before them and tiny bells tinkling from their wrists and ankles.

And, so that these lovely dancers were visible to the guests, the large domed room was lit by numerous torches.

To pretty the chambers for the feast, Cinaed deduced that many decorations were to be put into play. There were to be plentiful dried boughs of the grand fir tree dotted strategically. Episodically, these same boughs might be tossed into the hearth's fire to boost the citrusy fragrance of the occasion. The walls and tables were to have diapensia flowers jotted all about. He loved this floral type most especially. They were a small cushion forming perennial evergreen shrub that had enough height, maybe up fifteen centimeters, that were so simply attractive. Increasing the flowers natural appeal, the oval, thick and toothless leaves of the plant were arranged in dense rosettes which highlighted the solitary white flower.

And then he considered the food; ah, the once ever delightful garnishments, meats, fruits, stew, savory dishes of all kinds, delicious sweets, nuts and glazed breads for dessert.

His favorite heavy dish had been one called Haggis. It was a blend of heart, liver and the lungs of a sheep or calf and was minced with suet, onions, oatmeal and seasonings. The mixture was then boiled in the stomach of the animal chosen with that animal's abdominal lining laid over the rounded interior of the cauldron within which it was heated. Even now, the juices there enticed him. The hearty taste of the meat and their blended flavors drew him. The oatmeal created the texture of delicious sludge which made his stomach groan in anticipation and satisfaction; anticipation forever and satisfaction never. Or so he imagined.

There would also be wheat and barley porridges, cheese and milk from the cow and the goat. Brassica, cabbage and parsnips crammed in with the huge amount of dishes presented.

The fruits were likely to be raspberries, blackberries, strawberries and imported delicacies as well. He expected there to be pears, apples and other ripened bounty of the gods. Hazelnuts and slivered almonds were to be found amongst the victuals. The latter were searched for far and wide and were of such scarcity that they were used inconspicuously and as rare garnishment.

Honey was draped lavishly over so much.

And he laughed aloud at the beverages that were to be offered in abundance. The zythos, the mead and the caramel colored ale was to be amply supplied; poured into hollowed out horns for all.

As a last touch, henbane, a hallucinogenic plant was to be obtainable in very small and measured amounts. It had to be requested before it was to be shared. And those individuals requesting the powerful drug were to be closely observed and tended to in an emergency.

The significant persons engaged in this triumphant activity included he and Aiobheean, Catrione and Eumann, Constantine, Cinaed's henchman, lords and ladies of his royal entourage, Drust, Brude, Kynat and Bruide, their seconds and anyone accompanying those lords and their aids. And then there was the clergy. A few sycophants were welcome too. And then the rest.

It was to be a swirling mass of rowdy and happy folk, ranked high and some middle.

The rabble was responsible for itself.

Cinaed was the master of the far northern British Isles; all of it. And it was called Alba. It was never to be relinquished in his lifetime.

CHAPTER 39

One After Another

Five years and five more children later, King Cinaed and his treasured queen, Aiobheean, were locked deeply in reminiscences of the incredibly pivotal period of his formal takeover of Alba.

They were not discussing politics, certainly not. They chortled over the idea that all of Alba in eight forty three was speculating upon who the mysterious queen was who had been presented to the public officially on that very eve of his coronation.

They lay side by side, heads in palms, on their expansive bed, brimming with good humor about how the unknown Aiobheean had been then.

As if in adolescent thrall, Cinaed gazed upon his partner with all the adoration that he had aimed her direction when he was actually a youth. She amazed him and maintained her status as his heart's true and singular desire to this day. He was starkly aware of the rarity of any man in such a raw epoch as this one for establishing lifelong fidelity to one woman.

That had never been a choice for Cinaed from that fateful moment when he first partook of the glory of Aiobheean; before he knew her name even. He had, in a haze, shadowed her to the edges of Loch Fyne. And, astoundingly, she had received him with open arms and then followed with her delicious widespread legs. He had known nothing of love then, miraculously and barely having survived his trial towards manhood and then had been shot through with perplexity when he viewed her. His vision of Aiobheean had animated him into a state of fevered hope and he had loved her unstoppably since.

He had foolishly, in his immature ignorance, spurned her; but, bless the gods, the one God, for permitting their chance encounter at the Abbey. He honestly had Eumann to thank for that evermore. His life had been resurrected then and he was eternally grateful.

Had reuniting with Aiobheean been worth it he reflected in truly meaningless reflection. The answer was so glaringly obvious that the question need never truly be asked. He raised it simply so that he was able to assess her value to him repeatedly. He craved promenading through this emotional and mental terrain of his regarding her marvelous qualities.

Was she worth it he repeated once again to himself?

She was loved by the Alban commoner once the wraps of her mystery had been peeled away from her identity. She behaved consummately and it was not feigned whatsoever. She was naturally a woman and person primed to perform acts of empathy, charity and goodwill as she reached for the better welfare of one and all. She was not capable of controlling herself when it came to caretaking of others.

What he enjoyed the most in this daydream of his was using it and his eyes to tick off accolades of her physical beauty. He went back to this over and over. He was obsessed but that was the sum total of what love was about. It never failed to achieve an aria of pulse within both his heart and his manhood.

Where to start then?

She was two years his senior at age thirty nine and she still set his body aflame and afire. Incredibly, and she was hardly conscious of this, certainly was never arrogant about it, her frame was ever lean. Her softness of flesh had remained smooth and her buttocks and hips had not thickened an iota since Eumann had led him to her in the Abbey's principle entry room.

Again incredibly, he thought, and his cock predictably roused at this, her breasts had enlarged more so. She had such largesse there initially when twenty one but since they had enlarged in size considerably. It defied all the mechanics of the majority of mortals. It seemed her frame should have been helpless in carrying their weight; but her frame was strong and could and did. Her breasts were vastly curved and pendulous; but the fall of her flesh was minimal and the rise of her mounds perfectly offset and balanced one another.

She was not self-conscious of her breasts at all. They may have moved as she walked but she blithely ignored what others might have considered an impediment or encumbrance. Attitude was so much and her attitude did not dismiss her body but did not dwell on it either. She looked as she did; it was there and that was all.

Their further filling had occurred indisputably over the years as they had stayed permanently swollen from the suckling of her five babes on them since his coronation. And she also had had her children one after the other without surcease.

Constantine had enjoyed assisting with the growth of his brothers and sisters. He had not continued his interest in the Church as it happened but imagined instead going into battle as was permitted at his age and presently desired to be a soldier in his father's early image. But for now he was with his family and took delight in his interaction with his brothers, Aed, Fergus and Tenegus as well as his play with his sisters Loern and Mael Muire. He did this until, just past his twenty first year, he found his own life mate.

Tonight, it was Cinaed's opportunity to suckle on Aiobheean's breasts and nipples. As Aiobheean spoke in an almost unnoticed murmured monologue of her remembrances, Cinaed released the ties at the back of her tunic. He discerned that she smiled as he did this, that she permitted his doing this and that she wanted it but maintained her ongoing blissful chatter as well.

He loosed and parted the corset-like top and he kissed the portions of her soft and supple back that were exposed. As he continued to kiss and lick her there, she raised her arms and he lifted the material over and off of her. Each and every instance he did this, as if it was always the first, her dense and glorious mounds bobbled for him and he then teased himself and her as he trailed his tiny kisses alternating with brush strokes of his lips up to the outer perimeter of one breast.

He let the heat of his breath and the tiny pressure and moisture of his lips arouse her.

Finally, as she always did, she peered down at his upwardly gazing eyes and she turned to him. She invariably cupped both of her breasts and squeezed them together, placing her two thick, long and hard nipples into his mouth at the same time. He licked them then and they were hot and she moaned loudly.

Precisely here, she inevitably held her chest to his supping lips and lashing tongue with one hand and dropped her other hand to his trew covered cock and balls. She rubbed his cockhead automatically as its length protruded from his under garment. He sucked her ongoing as he stripped off the short trew from his waist. Once past his ankles, he kicked it away.

She had massaged his dew into his skin and a sheen surrounded his plum colored, mushroom sized cockhead. The pleasure of her lengthening nipples and her erotic touch of his glans and frenulum were intense. His dew flowed some more.

He had to have her without hesitation. He swiftly but gently brought her supine and angled her legs outward. She panted in her excitement and he growled in an undertone of passion.

He edged his bulbous cockhead and thick, long shaft into her gradually. Unless she was desirous of a quick burn, he had to progress slowly into her. He straddled her legs and did something unique this episode.

As he plumed her depths, he took his strong legs and pushed her legs tightly together as he kept driving into her. He was too in need to realize why but he did this nonetheless.

This created an oasis of excruciatingly pleasurable sensation as it compressed the area of their union and his cock felt her vault more thoroughly and her clit vibrated much more intensely than ordinary.

Their anticipation for release escalated wildly. He pumped her hard, fast and deep without regard to her wishes. It just so happened that her ardor was being specially fulfilled by these very movements of his.

Their bodies rocked vigorously, her moans were continuous now. He grunted with a bottomless passion and close approach to his threshold's trigger. By only seconds, Cinaed rocketed first into his hot jets of splashing pearly ejaculate onto the walls of her core.

When Aiobheean experienced his storming liquid thuds upon her inner vault, a vibrant, unbroken cry escaped her lips. Her hips involuntarily lifted as did her head. Her body shook with spasm after spasm of waves spiraling over his thick column and she clutched him, held him and then he sensed the mild gouge of her fingernails as blood seeped from where she had scratched him.

Minutes later, she tasted his blood from her fingers and painted the same metallic taste over his lips.

"We have had our children, my love. Turn me, oh please turn me!"

He commanded her to remove the silver choker that she had worn in his stead.

She let it slip off the bed where the henchman later found it; and wore it as he had prior.

It was in this moment that Cinaed complied with her wish.

CHAPTER 40

Columba Impresses Him

Cinaed and Aiobheean, as two vampires should, were supremely active in this year. Aiobheean was so fortunate to have many women to aid her in the raising of their children as she and Cinaed vanished during each day. Only Catrione, Eumann and the henchman were privy to why this was. No one asked as no one questioned the King.

As the only human of the five, the henchman ruled within certain established guidelines in the hours of sun and daylight.

So, Aiobheean, when in motion, tended to their daughters and sons whose ages spanned from one to five years old. And there was nothing quite as involving as raising a bundle of very young humans, even with help! And all five, oddly enough, had been born without a hint of the undead within them.

In the meanwhile, Cinaed was shepherding two massive projects of his own besides governing in those perpetual routine matters. The undead spirit residing inside him was often chagrined at his leniency and even handholding with the Church but he, as with all breathing beings, had to submit to the mysteries of existence periodically. And so, he ground his teeth and submitted also. And he well knew that probing for answers to his or others behavior was often a fruitless task that was simply better left alone.

So, what were the projects that so effectively absorbed the King?

He was engrossed as a builder of two monstrous stone structures. One was for himself and his retinue and the other was to bring the Columban Church into a closer fold; a fold that was proximate to him rather than flung to the Isle of Iona. Iona was isolated and far away. He wished for neither of these circumstances.

Hold thy enemy close.

The primary issue, though, was where he, Aiobheean, his family, his mother and Eumann were to settle. Not that he had tired of Scone's Abbey but he relished a fortress that he was able to call his own. He no longer chose to dwell in an annex, even if beautiful, of an abbey. He had grown accustomed to the ever presence of the monks finally. And yes, they had given him support in crucial times. But he did not desire to ask permission of anyone in his own abode anymore.

A grand beast of a building had gone up in Forteviot then. It was within a twelve hour journey of either Scone or Dunkeld. He was to name this new citadel of his, merely, the Palace of Forteviot.

And the reasons for the concern with its juxtaposition to Scone and Dunkeld were because Aiobheean's parents had selected Scone as their permanent residence. And the Cathedral at Dunkeld was soon to be completed and was to become the fresh center of the Columban Church.

He was not only in the process of finalizing the first ever cathedral at Dunkeld but had pressed the Ionian devotees of Columba to remove their center from that isle. There was resistance but he was King. And Columba had sincerely impressed him he was loath to say to himself. That he and that Saint's church must stand shoulder to shoulder, toe to toe geographically was very important to Cinaed.

He felt a sadness that, upon transfer of his capitol from Scone to Forteviot, his henchman would not follow or continue his duties for Cinaed. He was ready to seek his own fortune separate from Cinaed and mingle once more with his kin who mainly dwelt in the central lowlands of the region south of where Cinaed reigned. It was known as Galloway and he was headed there.

Cinaed was momentarily hard pressed to find a substitute his worthy.

As a gift to this savvy and trusted lieutenant of his, Cinaed permanently bestowed the silver choker upon him. It was a very generous action for Cinaed to have performed as the choker had vast value in and of itself but also had huge value as a token of the love shared between him and his queen. Yet neither he nor Aiobheean were able to touch or wear it, so let the man have it!

The most delicate element of accomplishing the geographic alteration of the Church was that of bringing the fragile relics of Saint Columba to the just minted cathedral in Dunkeld. In addition, the Irish Columban's sought those relics as well.

The Irish Columbans and the Columban representatives of Cinaed had met over the matter. Nothing was gained by this assemblage until, miraculously, the two opposing groups decided to cooperate with each other and share the relics. At what became the turning point for all present, negotiations were greatly simplified and flowed forward smoothly after that.

To Cinaed, the bones of the Saint were the most precious of the relics in Ionian possession. So he had previously had a reliquary crafted and upon the viewing of the object by the gathered monks, the Irishmen deferred and gave Cinaed Columba's bones. As Cinaed later called it, and he called it many things, the Monymusk reliquary assured them mightily of the bone's sheltered protection within.

Those same Irishmen took the remainder of Columba's lesser relics to their homeland shortly thereafter.

This reliquary, which housed those much ossified bones, was to be the vessel for transferring those bones from Iona to Dunkeld and was also to be taken into periodic battle in service of Alban victory, had to be a strong and solid box. This box which contained such sainted bones had to be magnificently created.

Cinaed went to great lengths to insure that was what occurred. He had ordered that its design be of a combined wood and metal construction. It was to have the influence of a multitude of artisans, Pictish and Gael most especially.

The casket was formed of thick wood and its interior was covered in a linen fabric throughout. The portions of the casket that required metal and the bottom, sides and lid of the object were hammered by Angle and Saxon smiths from an iron and copper alloy.

When finished, it appeared as if it was a miniature house. Its precise measurements, as Cinaed had asked for these exactly, were one hundred twelve millimeters in width, fifty one millimeters in depth and eighty nine millimeters in height.

Cinaed had demanded that the lid and front plate contain a field of spots with leaping European wildcats biting at their tails. He had despised these animals since his near encounter with death by one. To have that be the animal on the reliquary chasing and injuring itself pleased Cinaed to the utmost.

His slang for the contraption, replete with Columba's bones, as monks bore it forward into battle at his command, was that of Brecbennoc of Saint Columba. To Cinaed, the reliquary was that "pointed thing" that he took to battle only as God's protection over his soldiers.

And now it was securely tucked away in the Dunkeld Cathedral.

And let his bones forever remind us, Cinaed ironically thought, of all that might be right upon the world were we to trust our light within.

CHAPTER 41

Gone Once More

Aiobheean and Cinaed often were fortunate just to have brief contact in passing as their evenings and involvements rushed by. They kissed quickly and then she hurried to take over the children's caretaking. He hustled out to find the henchman who had replaced the old. He was anxious to hear from his lips the progress stirring amongst the stones of Forteviot and Dunkeld.

This particular mingling with the new lieutenant struck Cinaed oddly. He peered at the man's neck subtly, repeatedly, as they conversed. The absence of the choker there had revived his reminiscences of the choker's origins; when he had youthfully first gazed upon it and Aiobheean.

Its absence reminded him of how their lives had changed so drastically since. And that prompted him on several levels. One was to quickly scan his mind and use his undead tool of sight to scrutinize, momentarily, the world of his youth. He had not done this since he had sallied forth from Dal Riata toward Scone. The review was instantaneous and thoroughly grey in nature. The second level was to command a span of time with Aiobheean to discuss this very matter and it's enlarging concern that had suddenly taken seed within him.

For some days now, he had been plagued with fleeting episodes of dizziness. Each one was followed by a faint tremor of his hands. Finally, the spot sitting just above the bridge of his nose would pulse enough so that he perceived its exact location. If he pressed it long and hard enough to depress his skin there slightly, the mild but building ache to his head would quickly disappear. Otherwise, the throb remained with him a while.

He tore himself away from his second in search of Aiobheean. His new man was as trustworthy as his last, though for slightly different reasons Cinaed smirked. He had to be. Cinaed had frightened him with the threat of certain death if he were to ever disregard or attempt to harm Cinaed or his undead queen or mother and his advisor, Eumann, in their sleep.

And besides, this man appreciated Cinaed's far reaching abilities as well. He was in awe of Cinaed. Trust was to have been the best solution but that kind of grooming took its own sweet time; and there had not been this luxury whatsoever.

There was an area in the Annex that was strictly off limits to the males unless it was the King. He was free to go anywhere he pleased. So he strode in to the nursery and quickly spied Aiobheean as she had their youngest babe, Aed, suckling at her plentiful nipple.

The other children were actively engaged with the royal nannies that tended to the needs of his four elder children.

Cinaed spoke to these nannies. "For the next hour, take your charges, our children, to other areas if you will." As these women scurried about to do his bidding, Cinaed found each of his youngsters and gave them all a deep pucker on their forehead. He loved them as they loved him.

Once the area was cleared and it was just he, Aiobheean and Aed on her teat, Cinaed began. "My sweet Queen, I have need of your wise thoughts here and now."

Aiobheean switched Aed to her other quite lengthy nipple for the babe to suckle as the first nipple was turning sore. This babe sucked her with the same urgency of Cinaed and, to her, it was delightful. But as the time passed, she felt the tenderness of her flesh creep up on her.

Cinaed envied the tiny lad as he wished that his mouth were presently attached to her glorious crinkled tip.

Aiobheean innocently cut into his reverie. "I am completely at your behest my love and am listening to you intently."

Cinaed placed his lips upon her forehead as he had done with the children. He also chucked Aed under the chin but that did not slow the babe on his mother's teat not a wee bit. "My seer's vision gave me concern earlier. Use yours and focus too on Dal Riata, your youthful home, the tunnel, the Loch and tell me what it is that you see as you do that."

"Most assuredly love. You are obviously concerned."

Allow me to go there for a minute."

"Of course my love, please do that."

Aiobheean's eyelids flew wide open after a brief pause of eyelid closure. "That cannot be, Cinaed! Let me describe it as I see it.

My parent's house, my little girl's space and all in the wheelhouse are empty or abandoned; and abandoned for a lengthy period. I am surprised, shocked, appalled at its condition!

And the tunnel, the tunnel of Eumann, your mother and eventually you has partially collapsed. It is not only impossibly dangerous now but the entrance has fallen in too. That entrance, because of this, is blatantly exposed. But that is of no matter as no one resides within its proximity. The area is in ruins. What is it that could possibly have happened to what once existed in Dal Riata?!"

"Look to the Loch as well, love. Look where we first met. It has changed greatly also. See it for the moment."

Again, Aiobheean paused with eyelids tightly squeezed together. She actually gasped this time. "It's as if a forest has grown upon its shore. When observing it from the shell of the city, it's apparent that the Loch and its perimeter have gone untended at length!"

"Yes my Queen, Dal Riata is in slow decay and soon to be rapid ruin as it is overgrown and left without its citizenry.

We must go there tonight.

We must transform and ply the clouds to our beloved, once thriving, and beautiful city. We cannot stand idly by and allow Dal Riata to cease to be!"

Cinaed called for the nannies return. Aiobheean gently handed the blanket wrapped Aed to one of the caretakers.

Aiobheean's nipples continued to drop liquid upon Aed's departure and then abruptly ceased their flow.

Aiobheean and Cinaed ambulated as fast as was dignified to their royal chambers. Cinaed waved their retinue away and they all fled immediately.

The pair was tipping toward their winged transformation when Cinaed trembled and then seized. It started as his eyeballs rolled back and his knees plunged him to the floor when they collapsed beneath him. Had she not caught his arch downward, he would have smacked his forehead soundly upon the stone surface.

The light from the burning hearth revealed, as if in a dream for her, the ripples of muscular spasm that assaulted Cinaed's eyelids, his torso and his four limbs. He drooled copiously and his teeth chattered. There was seeping blood from where the edges of his teeth had slightly pierced his tongue.

She held him as if to never let him go.

She rocked him and rocked him, cooing his name and that she sorely loved him repeatedly.

His master had usurped any and all control that Cinaed had possessed.

This master drew the undead spirit from the womb that was Cinaed; his fleshly home for many a year now.

It was his home no longer. He was compelled, almost assaulted, in his master's wish for him to leave Cinaed's bosom and fly to regions beyond the shrouded horizon. So into the black the ancient undead one thrust himself. He had done this in eight eighteen from out of the Uamh on Am Monadh then.

It was eight forty eight, thirty years later, and he was gone once more; whipped on the tidal currents of the sea of air surrounding him.

He heard the cacophony, the insistent shrieking of his master. This noise was to stop when he settled in that unknown locale; a locale known by his master only.

His huge webbed wings thrashed. They took him far from Cinaed.

When he reached his necessary cave, he was unaware of where he was. He felt that it was warmer and gentler than the northern British Isles.

It was in the verdant Spanish hills.

CHAPTER 42

Do Not Leave Me

As the spasmodic motion that manifested itself into waves throughout Cinaed's body subsided, Aiobheean maintained her loving embrace in spite. She, even as vampire, had zero inkling of what Cinaed was suffering from.

There was not a vampire in existence that understood the modes of the ancient one. He was the oldest and from him sprang a lineage of sacred individuals experiencing eternal life. And he had no undead peer who equaled the seer abilities that he wielded; although even he had limitations in that realm. He was restricted in other regards too. His restrictions were minor in their comparison with his undead kin.

This touched Aiobheean thoroughly in that she twisted upon ignorance's pole because she did not even begin to have a concept of the ancient one's true powers. That there was undead spirit strong enough to move in and out of human beings; that notion was not only foreign to her but beyond what her imagination was capable of conjuring up.

She was shattered, therefore, by what was happening to her lifelong love. That Cinaed was simply being disinhabited would have been utterly stupefying to her.

She believed that he was dying. She found herself writhing in an emotional nightmare. She recognized that vampires did not die, not like this anyhow. Yet here Cinaed was, in her estimation, dying before her very eyes. And she was helpless to aid him in his gravest moment of need. That he was being pitched back into human dimension and was no longer like her was inconceivable.

Yet, as she clutched at him and he began to recover, her fear of his death faded. He was, thankfully, not about to die.

And why, of a sudden, was she adept at peering into his actions where she had never before been able? Again, that the ancient being that had resided within Cinaed just moments ago was no longer blocking her vision of Cinaed's past did not occur to her whatsoever. She just knew that she now observed Cinaed powerfully.

This newfound sight had halted instantly with other things as her mind processed the particular unfolding images of interest presented to her. Anything else was inconsequential and she paid it no heed.

Why was Cinaed's mother so prominent in what she was visualizing? The sense was of a celebration long ago. And she was nowhere within the stream of these images now racing through her synapses. She shook her head gently to try to find a way to clear these images. Maybe it just took a shake of the head. Aiobheean saw these disturbing images still.

In these images, Catrione was under the influence of mead it appeared.

Her figure was lush as always and was contained within seductive raiment.

He hated his mother then but there he was. It was her king, her husband, her lover, Cinaed.

And he was staring at his mother's dancing, undulating form before him. Was he equally drunk as she was? Did it matter?

And then, what did Aiobheean see? She did not want to see this but was in the grips now of an obsession that was beyond her.

The soft bulge at Cinaed's crotch was ever enlarging. He even stroked over it. It was apparent that he attempted to withhold those strokes but could not.

Wickedly, Catrione approached Cinaed closely and bent to him. She held her breasts to him.

Aiobheean was aware that Catrione, though short and small, had breasts nearly Aiobheean's size. They always seemed huge on the otherwise tiny woman. This occasion was no exception.

And she cupped these breasts of hers and served them to Cinaed. He licked at her pressing nipples through the material at Catrione's bodice. They may have only been tongue darts but his action upon her could not be denied now or ever.

Aiobheean's sight trailed them to a room of their own.

This could not be! She was rapt but horrified; his own mother, her own son! No matter the mead, this was shameful!

Aiobheean froze in disbelief as she probed Cinaed's mind further; all the while he was gradually regaining consciousness in her arms and her lap.

She shrank from him as she witnessed more of this past episode of incest.

It was in this private room that mother and son enacted a ritual that was incredibly taboo. And Aiobheean was privy to the minutest of detail.

That he entered Catrione with a swollen cock and that they felt the passion that was rightfully reserved for others, not them, truly shattered Aiobheean!

She had deemed herself lost and broken minutes ago at Cinaed's collapse but what she experienced now was an altered destruction for her. This was the telescoping inward of her heart into the tightest shimmering dark star of disdain, repulsion, betrayal and anger that tore at her very soul.

And he had not had the courage to have ever told her either. And she detected a remnant of his thought that she would have accepted this! How he did not know her as it turned out!

She might have been willing to forgive him and his mother had he ever informed her of this happening. He would have probably been able to mollify her based on the fact that Aiobheean was not in his life then; but only if he had confessed his escapade to her.

It was not his mother's place to reveal their intertwining to her either. It was his obligation and his alone! And he had not! She would not have that and would not permit him to touch her evermore. She was absolutely done with him!

She did not understand; did not desire the understanding.

It was then that she slid out from beneath Cinaed's head. He roused while she stood.

He, no matter the blur that occluded his eyes, was so cognizant that she was departing him forever.

"Do not leave me my love! Whatever is the cause, I beg of you, hear me out on any or all issues that you find distressing!"

She said not a word to him and left him lying in his drool on the bed chamber floor.

Her children were better off here than where she was going as she knew not where that was. She planned to return and raise her children her own way if at all possible.

She transformed and the might of her wings almost created the illusion that she was being sucked out into the night.

He wept then and hardly had energy or balance to sit. He was no longer able to mutate into bat form either. He had that one figured as he was no longer vampire.

He was saved by the commotion and his cries as he wept.

His mother was the first to respond.

And she did what any vampire mother would have done for a son in the distress of the damned.

She turned him and he became undead again.

He attempted to follow Aiobheean but she blocked his sight and he did not have any idea of what path to take.

CHAPTER 43

Pictish Vanishing

The vampire entity, imprisoned within the softly covered domed hills here, had burrowed deeply into his temporary Spanish tomb. Who had an idea of the length that he was to have to twiddle his no longer corporeal thumbs in this thankless darkness? Feeding in the dreary perpetual curtain that often set a harsh pall from sunset to sunrise was his single truly exciting activity until he was directed into some human body again.

Oh, to someday see the light of day! He never had and had no idea as to how he ever would.

Sigh.

The cruel reality of being the King of the Undead was that he had a severe price to pay.

He perked up a bit though. A fragment of curiosity had lodged in him momentarily and he chose to mentally peek where it led him.

He had sheltered here for a good century now. This was how he might best idle away the months, the years and then the decades until he was encouraged by his master to exit his hole.

This is what the ancient one discerned as the ninth century flowed into the tenth. And lo, he was back in Alba in his mind. That mysterious land had called him and he eagerly went to it.

He attempted to never be shocked but was utterly. His mind did not require much of a view of the region to be informed of the grave decline of Dal Riata. This mental flight of his, from a height without detail of any sort, revealed to him that the city and its environs had been decimated; decimated not by force but by Mother Nature's force upon the city center and many structures surrounding with the exit of its people. It thrived no more. Buildings were in neglected collapse, paths and the few stone avenues that had existed were grown over or pushed aside by the grass, the weeds, the brambles and shoots of trees muscling upward. The Loch was hidden as its perimeter had been thoroughly encroached upon by saplings and young fir.

Dal Riata was a loss. He guessed that it would be completely taken by the wild and natural flora soon. In fifty to one hundred more years it was to be as if the city had never existed.

Villages did dot the proximate territory but this particular city, where he had transposed Eumann into undead form, was not salvageable.

The entity's sadness gripped him as that realization stormed his senses.

He honed his seer capacities down now to the details of person, property and geography as if he were an actual individual treading on the ground's surface. He was no longer overhead at this stage of his curiosity's probing and his senses and images had narrowed considerably.

He now heard conversations, the ringing sound of metal on metal as a smith worked over the shoe of a horse, the bark of the dogs that padded up the various paths and muddy roadways crisscrossing one another. He was close enough to the inhabitants and was relieved to find that activity of all kinds and varieties stirred the surface of this land.

His darkened impression of Dal Riata's fallen status was lightened by being in the mix of waves of motion and industry. Only one special place was radically changed for him but that had not weakened the heart of this civilization. For that, he was glad.

As a matter of fact, his concern for Dal Riata as a symbol of the Gael's progress was highly unnecessary. The life and culture of the Gael was in abundance and all about him.

He listened and Gaelic and Latin speech were shouted, whispered, laughed and cursed in almost universally. The Columban Church spread its tentacles everywhere. The carvings, the drawings, and the architecture that he espied everywhere were Gaelic.

What of the majority of the customs? Were they Gaelic as well?

So he then pressed his vision for more thorough observations and viewed even the lines of inheritance and entitlement. And he was abashed to discover that in the tussle between the genders for rightful and equal involvement socially, the female had been overcome. He knew that this occurred everywhere but that women had predominated somewhat with the Picts made it feel quite worthy and exceptional.

Matrilineal succession was now null and void as the hand of patrilineal succession smacked down hard upon the former.

Catrione, a presently wandering Catrione, must have been righteously resentful of this. In these times, her Pictish rank as princess meant nothing. As a vampire though she probably cared not; had she been human, she would have cared tremendously!

And the entity's insight was growing, enlarging and multiplying with example after example of Gael dominion. It was not the Gaels who were at risk! They may have given up one city but they had gained a lush and fruitful kingdom instead.

Stunned again in his rethinking, he groaned as the dark pool of energy sitting in a dark cave that he was. The Gaels were not in jeopardy whatsoever. It was, by god, the Pictish way that was fundamentally threatened. And the Pictish ethos was about to be cast down not by war, violence or treachery, but in the everyday acts of two cultures grinding together. It was the Pictish traditions that were becoming pulverized in this slow, persistent and rigorous process over time.

He searched and did not find individuals who bore woad tattoos in all the fleshy nooks and crannies that the Pictish had once done. The shorter stature and naturally dark locks of the Pict existed, yes; even so, a pale blond appearance with height aplenty had developed into preponderance by far. His vision also revealed a majority of blue eyes where there had been uniformity of number with brown before.

In this moment of recognition, the entity cried for his former times and wonderful companions. And Pict had been as critical for that as had been Gael.

The Pictish culture, obviously, was vanishing.

But why?

He had clout, a seer's vision and experience beyond the reckoning. But he still was only able to guess at the decline of the Pict.

It was gradual foremost. The treason would have doomed the Picts instantaneously if successful. But the

224

treason never occurred. He loved Aiobheean so much for that. The Picts, simply, were assimilated; they were absorbed by a more dominant Gaelic culture.

And what did this dominance entail, the amorphous creature asked himself? Several principle factors were at play he believed.

He deemed the Latin and Gaelic language joined had overwhelmed the tongue of the Pict. He was convinced that this was aided by the acceptance of the Columban Church by both the Gael and the Pict. The unanimous acceptance of Columba and his teachings forced the druids to go a begging. And the language of the Church was in Latin. Latin predominated here even over Gaelic for a period. The Pictish language stood nary a chance against this heavy lingual artillery.

He further felt that the Church homogenized the two cultures and ultimately selected one over the other. The Church favored Latinate, the Irish and a male's viewpoint. Therefore, the Church favored the Gaels. The Picts submitted and converted to the Gael's culture as they had converted to Columba's Irish Catholic Church.

The irony, he surmised, was that so many had attempted to conquer the Picts by the heavy hand of violence. It had not happened. It happened quietly, by the heavy hand of the Church.

As to the artifacts of the Pict versus the Gael, both were transcendent and beautiful. But as the Picts surrendered their language, their body art, their lines of succession, their pagan spiritual beliefs, it was not difficult for them to offer up their art and social ways as well.

This is what the entity perceived. And he was wise if not always pleasant. He laughed at the understatement of his little joke upon himself.

The Pictish culture had simply been smothered.

And he was capable of undergoing guilt in this stage of his evolution. He knew that he had brought Cinaed to the united kingdom by preserving his life in that battle of eight and thirty four.

He alone was responsible.

And the Picts had perished.

CHAPTER 44

His Repose

He wanted to assess the smaller picture now. What of his cohorts, friends and enemies alike?

When he had been of flesh and blood, Eumann had been his first experience. He recalled his effort to be as enmeshed with Eumann as possible so that Catrione was to be convinced that it was her always lover performing his always beautiful acts upon her.

Where Eumann was, so was Catrione. Early on in his chamber of dripping stalagmites and stalactites, he had already observed that the vampire, King Cinaed, minus the entity's spirit of course, had quietly and cautiously directed the couple to take their leave of their royal quarters. Cinaed did this as he did not choose to have their pretense performed within the walls of his official residence. Life, undead life that is, was much simpler for Cinaed if he only had to invent his own aging. He had no desire to orchestrate theirs in addition.

If they just disappeared now and sojourned and waited for his eventual arrival, Cinaed was insured of several items. Firstly, no one would miss Eumann and Catrione's absence. Secondly, that he was fully capable of seeing himself through to his acted demise. He was uncertain as to whether they were as able as him in their theatric capacities.

To act for oneself was doable. To direct others was much less predictable. So, to reduce the unknown variables, he took control early and commanded their departure.

Eumann and Catrione had left one full-moon midnight.

It was only Cinaed now. He had previously explained his queen's fall and paralysis to the masses. That it was a sheer lie was not his concern for this moment. All had to be in order so he could carry out his best conceivable rule.

He told her parents of Aiobheean's abandonment without the pertinent details. He had demanded of them that they never speak of her again.

Of the children, Constantine was sullen in regards to her departure. Again, Cinaed did not tell him the truth here. And how could he? Constantine was not even privy to the undead machinations of his father or mother. And Cinaed did not desire his disappointment whatsoever beyond what had already occurred.

The younger children grieved but in time found solace, comfort and an entire new set of dreams in their nannies.

His retinue did as they were ordered; and that was to never blaspheme by uttering Aiobheean's name ever.

The henchman did the duties for Cinaed while Cinaed slept the sleep of the dead.

Cinaed's pretense was initiated as he enacted behaviors that were intentionally eccentric in the process of fooling others. He no longer participated in battle with his soldiers again. Constantine now fulfilled that role exclusively.

He wore an oversize hooded cloak always. No one saw anything of him except his upper face and a huge beard that grew in conjunction with his ever present mustache.

As the years passed, he found dyes to streak his facial hair grey and eventually color that hair completely grey throughout.

He had a cane made and leaned onto that staff of wood always. He gradually bent over as if his spine was contorting and he was at its mercy.

He practiced the gradual escalating rasp of his voice.

From all appearances, over a certain span of time, he had morphed into the posture and attitude of that of an old man.

The entity had found this scheme of Cinaed's to be rather convincing. If he had the limited capabilities of human beings, he too would have been duped by Cinaed.

Cinaed was a creature of many talents. What hung in the balance then was how Cinaed was to apply those talents.

Miraculously, he performed wisely and well in the latter years of his leadership.

He wrote his code of laws and they were decreed.

He finished the two projects that he had cherished when Aiobheean, Catrione and Eumann had resided with him. Of the pair of projects, Dunkeld's Cathedral was established before the palace, the entity knew. The reliquary was transferred to the bowels of the cathedral with all due haste. Columba's old bones were a sought after spiritual commodity and the contraption's securitization was of prime urgency.

He then appeased the resistant Columban adherents by not only building plush quarters for them throughout the spiritual hallways but was determined to allow all superior Columban representatives with significant issues requiring royal sanctions or solutions to have free and instant access to the King himself. As he no longer rode with his armies on the battlefields north and south, he was ever available to the venerable religious authorities.

They were ever grateful and the long, tedious and difficult transfer of all items of the Faith from Iona to Dunkeld was forgiven the King and quickly forgotten. The Church became his strong ally and he theirs.

Close on the heels of this triumphant accomplishment, the Palace of Forteviot laid its last stone and was habitable and luxuriously presentable. Cinaed bade his Abbey-mates good bye and with a flourish of many thanks on his lips he exited to the Palace that was to be his home for the remainder of his life.

Of course, the ancient entity chuckled benignly at the idea of a vampire dying of natural causes. It did not happen and it was not about to happen at Cinaed's presumed demise.

The Palace housed a vampire imposter who was to live on for centuries, possibly even millennia. And, in the process, he would locate his mother and Eumann, cavorting with them over large swaths of time.

The entity actually appreciated Cinaed as Cinaed had served him well. Quite possibly this was just some pique on his part that Cinaed was free to roam and he was not. The envy cut viciously and created a ragged wound. It was so inexplicably and ruthlessly unfair of his master. Yet his master always had his reasons; it was never random.

Added to the list of deeds that were to pad Cinaed's legacy was the fact that, against his old enemies, he took territory in multiple clashes and expanded the borders of his control. He held these gains throughout his reign. This all as the Danes, Northumbrians, Angles and Saxons attempted to take back their lost ground from him.

He did make incursions into deeper southern areas in particular that he never was victorious over. This was Lothian country and he tried to take their cities and villages a half dozen times. Cinaed was repulsed with each new strike against them. After the sixth effort, he ceased his yearning for control and dominion over these peoples.

By middle February of eight and fifty eight years after the birth of Christ, Cinaed was tired of his role and blazingly ready at last to put an end to the charade and feign his death.

So, it was on precisely February thirteenth of that year that he closed his eyes as King for the last time. He did this under the archways of his Palace, in the deeper chambers at Forteviot.

The entity saw that they later claimed that a tumor of the brain took fast hold of him and buried him beneath its spread.

The entity did not require his vision to discern readily that the tumor was bogus and though future historians knew not, they had to attach some speculative cause to his passing.

He had made no requests regarding the site for his burial. He had trended eastward his entire life. Ironically, his corpse was taken westward to the isle of his birth, the Isle of Iona.

The nation of Alba was grieving for their hero and unifier. A saying was generated by the common man who loved him.

"Because Cinaed with many troops lives no longer
There is weeping in every house;
There is no king of the worth under heaven
As far as the borders of Rome."

He was deified by his country and history promulgated his rule as tidal and significant.

But it came as absolutely no surprise when his ancient perception, of a dim and pitch-black early morning, beheld the soil above King Cinaed's final resting place to mound upward, the earth there pushed away and Cinaed himself rise from out of the dirt sublimely; easily.

He gave no backward glance, took to the heavens and found his mother and her lover soon thereafter.

The cave bound entity smirked as Cinaed's repose was short-lived.

CHAPTER 45

After Cinaed

Much occurred in a generation or two after Cinaed removed his kingly raiment.

One odd occurrence arising in the entity's current time of nine hundred fifty eight Anno Domini, exactly one hundred years after Cinaed went his way, was that of Latin's entrenchment in the tongue of the common man. As the Columban Church became ubiquitous upon the landscape of Alba, the dialect of the Church found its way into frequent usage; and not just by monks but by the average citizen.

And there was a Latin term that was revived in the parlance. In fact, its usage was spreading so wildly and rapidly that it had begun to encroach upon the appellation for the country of Alba.

The word Scotia was initially proposed by the Romans for the tribes north of Hadrian's Wall who were not Irish or Gaelic. They were separate. And the derivation of that word, Scotia, meant just that, a separate people. Yet in the period of Septimius and the last of the Roman presence there, the entity having lived as flesh then, he recalled that word flowing off the tongues of his soldiers.

Then though, the word lapsed into nonexistence and was not spoken again.

Until now.

Latin was the cause.

The word was remembered again. It felt soft and correct to say. And it shot into everyday parlance. And finally, this term expanded and overtook the appellation of Alba; and Alba converted to Scotland.

Wise as he was, the entity perceived that the title was of lesser importance. Whether it was dubbed Alba or Scotland, it applied to the same land, the same people and the same spirit of those people. He murmured to himself, "What's in a name?"

The land had been joined together by Cinaed. Call that land what you will. Cinaed had been its first king. So went the thinking of the ancient one.

What he was truly interested in was the cast of characters who took the stage after Cinaed.

Subsequent to Cinaed, his half brother, Donald was handed the scepter. He had little to no impact on the land. He maintained the borders as they had stood for Cinaed upon his passing. That was the extent of it though. When he died of natural causes, his death was no pretense and he was most certainly dust.

Constantine ascended to the preeminent position and felt entitled as he had mastered the art of warfare and had been the strategic and actual genius behind the expansion of Scottish territory under his father. It had gone well for him and those who fought with him.

He was a kind and decent leader when not confronting those whom he wished to overthrow. He treated his usually conquering warriors with maximum care and concern as they were his brothers.

He had no children of his own but seemed unconcerned of that. He loved his queen and they were content.

He ruled for nineteen beneficent years.

He was never aware that his parents had devolved into vampires and that they still remained upon the land. And that was just as well.

As he desired, Constantine died in battle in eight and seventy seven.

His brother, the now grown Aed, followed in Constantine's footsteps.

His brothers Tenegus and Fergus served as brave and successful warriors alongside Constantine and then the same with Aed.

Their sister's married prominent men of proximate regions. One married a Northumbrian and one a Strathclyde lord. This cemented all their neighbors in both kinship and friendship and the consolidation of the Northern British Isles seemed likely.

Not likely the entity figured. Never enough blood shed no matter the appearances. He had much experience there.

And, no surprise, treachery prevailed. Aed, Tenegus and Fergus were brought to slaughter by a warrior peer whom all had trusted. Giric was his name and he quietly fomented rebellion among the ranks. He had ambitions to be king.

While King Aed, Tenegus and Fergus slept, Giric and his persuaded brethren picked off guards one by one and then stormed the royal chambers where the male Mac Alpins were ruthlessly slain.

The rough and tumble of this period stirred the entity not. His savage impulses bit into him as he observed these gruesome happenings. He was evolving but had yet to evolve thoroughly.

Giric, a descendent of Wrad, not only wrested control, he reigned for nearly a dozen years.

Bloodshed was perpetual and Giric died at the end of a sword in the Battle of Berthshire.

Often, the entity surmised appropriately that human beings did not require his encouragement to slay and slaughter. This they did rather well on their own.

It was at Giric's demise that the complexity of rotating rule and then death reached a pinnacle in this era.

Constantine the Second was Aed's offspring. Aed, so very close to his elder brother, had honored that brother with a namesake son.

This Constantine ruled in as significant a manner as his uncle had. Blood, plenty of blood was spilled; more so than before.

Red tainted everything. The entity pondered the notion of cooperation and compromise. Where had that mechanism gone? Was it the way of the matriarchy or had it simply never existed at all?

What he sensed in the here and now was a surfeit and excess of violent death. Even he, who fed on blood and death, was overwhelmed by its strength on occasion.

But this overriding nausea precipitated by the notion lasted but a second.

Constantine the Second was placed on the throne immediately after Giric was gored and gone.

The Danes then surged and pressed the Scottish for shed blood and land now. Would it ever cease? There was incessant arching of swords, sweeping of ancient cavalry at one another, coastal clashes at sea, spies, deceit and deception abounding.

There passed forty eight more years of human brutality for spoils and land.

After the Battle of Brinanburh in nine and thirty seven, the Saxon king Athelstan was victorious over Aed's son. Yet he spared the second Constantine on condition that the defeated king retreat from the battlefield forever.

In nine and forty three, Constantine the Second abdicated his throne and entered the monastery at Saint Andrews. He did not lift a sword again, he did not wear a crown again and he died at a ripe old age.

The boundaries of Scotland continued to ebb and flow the entity calculated.

But the land was never called any other than Scotland henceforward. Even now, the word Alba was rarely intoned. Soon it was to be near forgotten.

The entity waited some more.

About The Authors

Jeffrey Underwood graduated from the University of Washington with a degree in psychology. Though he has practiced as a Registered Nurse for many years, he comes from a family of published authors. His first published work was The Forbidden Tome; Hansel and Gretel's True Tale. His second was entitled Lethal Assumed; Lost Tome Found. This is his third effort at writing a tome but his first effort at true historical fiction. He currently resides in Mountlake Terrace, Washington, a suburb of Seattle and again hopes that those who read this third offering enjoy the time spent.

Kate Taylor collaborated with Jeffrey Underwood on this particular novel. Kate is nationally certified as an Activities Director. While she has worked in healthcare for many years and won awards for her service there, she is also talented in the world of watercolor and enjoys playing the piano. This work is her second serious effort at writing as her first work is entitled The Pink Eraser. She has contributed to books in the Activities profession. They say that no one lives in New Hampshire, but Kate does, and she has much in the way of writing to share. She hopes that all who read this tale of fiction and much fact will want for more.

Jeff and Kate met online and found that their collaborative interests meshed splendidly and this novel is the first example of that blending of gusto for writing that they certainly both have.